THE

SORTING

ROOM

Dear Ara,
Enjoy the story!
— Angelina Singer :)

Angelina Singer

To my mom and dad, who have always provided me with
everything I needed to follow my dreams <3

Cover art by Sara Freitas

2

VOLUME ONE:
THE MISTAKE

CHAPTER 1

The light pours in from an unknown source. She opens her eyes, trying to breathe but finding it difficult. The air is warm, with a subtle scent of mystery. She gains consciousness, and struggles to keep it. The small girl fights the obscurity she just left... existence is new to her. She has been born into the unknown, and is yet to find out what her intended role will be. Her rapid, strained breathing intensifies.

"Hi there... take it easy. You're just finishing gaining existence. Breathe. You're okay. You'll be okay..." She finally manages to keep her eyes open long enough to see a boy likely only a bit bigger than her, with short, pale blonde hair, bright blue eyes, and a kind smile. He's holding her small, frail, body against his much stronger one, likely as an attempt to comfort her. "It's a tough process. I remember my day of origin like it was yesterday... but according to my personal records, it's been about four hundred years, actually. But here, age isn't something we notice - we are all entered into existence in the likeness of a 20-year-old humanoid, and we don't visibly age at all. Anyway, you won't be able to speak clearly for another few minutes. Vocal faculties require a longer time to form. Wow, you have very clear eyes... a lovely violet, if I do say so myself. That's an *extremely rare* quality in Sorters..." Her confused expression makes him realize the gravity of the moment, and he slows down to try to accommodate her needs.

"My apologies, I should have realized that this is already a lot to take in, and the process is painful. The burning will subside in a moment. Just breathe... see, almost there. Good. Allow me to introduce myself. I am Onyx. I'll be your guide through the realm of the Upperworld." The girl slowly and hesitantly nods her head. "Uhhhhhhh.... hello?" "Hey, look at you - an overachiever. Three minutes in and you're already talking like a pro. I told you it would get better. And I bet the burning sensation has subsided too?" She nods her head again. "Good. Rest here in the utero chamber as long as you need." The small girl looks at him with eyes holding a thousand questions, a mind yet untapped in the universe of emotions and thought patterns that she has unwittingly entered. She slowly looks around at the stark white capsule-like enclosure she is in, with nothing but a blanket and this boy to talk to, or at least motion to. Her throat is still damaged from the burning sting of new life.

"That burning you felt was molecular bonding. This technology joins molecules at a rapid pace, which produces heat. An hour ago you were a speck about this big." An out-reached hand from Onyx shows her the distance between two fingers, supposedly meant to mimic her previously primitive state. "Ahhhhh... Ahhhhhh...." He clamps a soft white hand over her open mouth. "Slow down there, speedy. You'll speak when you're able to. Take it easy... you don't want to hamper your light-gathering process." She nods again, feigning understanding, likely not for the last time. "I promise I'll explain everything in a bit. You need to gain strength first. Until then, I will stay with you. Mark my words, little one - I won't leave you."

The frail little being looks up at him with thankful eyes, still mute but wholeheartedly grateful. The business of being something is a lot to handle... mere obscurity is infinitely easier but not nearly as important. And little did she know that she was about to embark on a brand new adventure, an eternal functionality that would likely serve her well, if she followed directions and learned well.

✳✳✳

Onyx falls asleep next to her in the chamber, and she allows herself to succumb to sleep as well. It offered at least a temporary obscurity, one that would bring some comfort to her spinning mind and heightened senses.

✳✳✳

The new arrival awakes to the soothing sound of the utero chamber buzzing, and her guide still stationed right next to her. "Hello there, little one. Glad to see you're awake. I'm pleased to tell you that you have completed the process of gaining existence. You may try to speak, if you like - your language faculties are fully developed now."

"Uh, hello... Onyx?" He couldn't hide his apparent smile. "Yes, you remembered! Quite the smart one, aren't you?" Her smile matched his immediately. "Do I have a name too?" Onyx grins. "That, my dear, is already ingrained in your DNA. Names here are quite important - they signal much about your future work. If you please allow me to scan the microchip in your right forearm, I'll let you know."

Without hesitation, the small girl exposes her pale arm to her new friend, which he gently holds in his own soft hand before shining a small red laser onto it. The light turns green and then beeps, with a name appearing on the screen. "Your name, little one... is Luna."

CHAPTER 2

"Luna? What does that mean?" Her eyes meet Onyx's with much confusion, but his are filled with all knowledge and calm. "That, you will discover in time. Even I haven't quite figured out the reason for my name... all I know is that Onyx is a black precious stone. I have no idea what relevance it has to me. I can tell you, however, that Luna refers to the moon, as evidenced in a 'lunar eclipse', for example. But again, irrelevant. It soon will be though - patience, little one."

Luna nods her head, awaiting her next instructions. "Uh, so... what do I do now?" "Well, when you feel strong enough, you can leave the utero chamber. Just let me know, and I'll let you out. Then I'll give you the grand tour of the Upperworld - there's much for you to see." Luna hesitates for a moment, but then decides to go ahead and move forward with the next phase. "Okay, I think I feel okay now. Can we go now?" Onyx nods his head excitedly. "Indeed, you've absorbed all the light you need to properly thrive. It's time. Come along now, I think you'll begin to see the importance of what you're about to embark on." And with that, Luna gets up, and Onyx leads her out of the utero chamber and into the Upperworld to explore the seemingly endless land stretching below them and the purple sky reaching for infinity above them.

✳✳✳

8

"Come along now, there is much to see. First, I'll show you to your living quarters. You'll be living in the New Arrivals District for your first hundred years. After that, you can move into the centennial neighborhood with the larger dwellings, where I live. We operate largely on a hierarchy here - don't take it personally, it's just how things are run." Luna nods her head. She continues walking into the dwelling complex neighborhood, following Onyx with much excitement. As far as she can see, rows and rows of large pink and blue pods are stationed in neat concentric circles, with various lights blinking and quietly beeping around them. As she's taking it all in, Onyx stops in front of one of the smooth, pink pods.

"This is your pod, Luna. To be granted access, just raise your right arm over the censor - that's your key in, and it is unique to you, and you only." Luna does as she is told, and the door slides open. "Well, what are you waiting for? Go on in." Onyx follows her in and then the door shuts behind them. "Here you will find enough supplies and amenities for you to live comfortably. There is food stocked in the kitchen, not that you need it - it's merely for pleasure, since we gain our nourishment solely from light. There is also a sleeping chamber over there, where you can recharge your light power anytime you feel the need to. And in there, you will also find suitable garments for you to wear - that way you can be rid of those plain fibers you were created in." Luna looks around at her new abode with wide eyes. "So, why is everything pink?" "Oh, it's a gender-based categorizing system. Similar to the humanoids, we are created with a distinct gender. Thus, since you are female, your home is pink. The blue ones are male. It allows us to keep track of how many of each kind we currently have in existence as we constantly increase in number." Luna seems to be satisfied with that answer, and runs her hand on the soft fabric of her sleeping chamber. "I still can't believe this is all for me?" Onyx nods his head. "It is, indeed. We want you to be as comfortable as possible living here with all of us."

Luna smiled, as she began to feel very welcome in her new home. "Can I try on some new clothes?" "Of course! They are all yours. Go on... I'll wait right here."

Onyx responds to the beeping from his wrist, the implanted communication device glowing a pale green. "Hello? Yes, she's doing just fine... I'll bring her there soon enough... I want her to get acclimated first... yes, I'll take care of it... I know... understood. Okay, I'll update you on her progress shortly... bye!"

Just as Onyx clicks off his device, Luna returns to the common room after dressing in a pale pink jumpsuit and white shoes, which appeared to glow in the effervescent light of her dwelling. "Well don't you look just fantastic. Okay, remember now that you can find your dwelling at any time by alphabetically walking through the new arrival portion of the pod grounds. Your name is Luna, so you will be stationed in the 'L' region, somewhere between Lucia and Luxe, in the twelfth concentric circle from the center. Now, tell me, little one -

are you feeling strong enough to continue? Or would you like to rest a bit more first?"

Luna shakes her head. "I… think I'm okay."

"Marvelous. Okay then. The time has come for you to meet Zephyr." Luna's unsure expression led Onyx to the realization that he ought to clarify himself in order to put her at ease. Her brand-new soul had no sense of security yet - it was his job to provide it. "Oh not to worry - Zephyr is kind, and a very wise soul indeed. He is also the all-powerful leader of this realm, but don't let that intimidate you. He just always likes to personally introduce himself to the new arrivals before… confusion develops -" "What?" Onyx stops short in his train of thought. "I've already said too much…"

CHAPTER 3

With Luna in tow, Onyx leads her out of her pod, and into the vast landscape of the habitation district. "Where are you taking me now?" "To meet Zephyr - it's important that you stay in good graces with him. He rules the Upperworld, and does so with wisdom and justice."

Luna still couldn't easily follow what he was referring to, but she resolved herself to follow him now and ask questions later. The urgency with which he was leading her clearly required that level of cooperation.

Before she knew it, they were leaving the habitation district and swiftly moving toward a large, stark white enclosed structure with a plethora of floating lights surrounding it. Spires and intricate architecture reach high into the atmosphere, higher than Luna's violet eyes can reach. Other beings were milling around, likely going about their daily business. But Onyx was leading her directly to this frightening structure. There was something so tangibly frightening in the level of its regality, and the sheer terror that surrounded it reflected this mood - even the purple sky had darkened into a foreboding halo.

"Right this way, Luna." Luna looks up to see Onyx motioning for her to follow him through the stark white door, his out-reached arm acting as the one-way path into her eternal, unknown future.

Upon entering the structure, Onyx leads her by her hand through a long hallway, with the immaculate flames of the lanterns nearly blinding her newly-formed eyes. Her dainty hand shields her from their blazing light, her breath caught in her throat as they walk. At the end of the long hallway, stood a large, black desk with a powerful being stationed directly behind it.

His piercing gaze was one of utter intensity - nearly boring through Luna's very soul. She is instantly intimidated. Instead of pale blonde hair like Onyx's or the darkest black like her own, he had bright orange flames dancing atop his head, casting little shadows bowing down to him around the grand hall. The excessively pale skin of his face is pulled taut, with a look of stress and pain in every fiber if his being. His pitch black eyes are sunken deep into his head, without an obvious iris or pupil - just mounds of utter blackness, his face rendered expressionless and harsh.

"Good day, Zephyr. I've brought with me one of our newest creations from utero batch number ten trillion, eight billion, twelve million, twenty-four thousand, nine hundred and eighty-seven. I present to you, Luna."

Luna fought hard to avoid cowering beneath his gaze - it was impossible not to flinch while he stared her down. "Come here, young spirit. Let me see you." Luna glances at Onyx. "Go on…" Onyx whispers with urgency, as if keeping him waiting would be deemed unacceptable. She forces her feet forward, her small frame approaching the largely imposing desk of Zephyr's preeminent power. "Closer…" he beckons her. Luna slowly continues walking right to the desk, eventually resting her small, white hands at the edge of the black desk, her clear violet eyes staring up at Zephyr's pitch black ones.

"Uh, hello." Zephyr's stare continues to bore into her very mind, foregoing the typical expectations of propriety in order to find out all about the new being he has welcomed into the realm. "Oh my darling, your eyes are... so unique. I've only seen that shade of violet in... a select few others. It's quite... prophetic." Luna struggles to remain calm under this unsettling thought, her feet nervously squirming under the weight of his eyes. "Oh, um, thank you?"

Zephyr glances in an exasperated fashion at Onyx, as if to say, *what kind of nuisance have you brought to me?* Onyx merely stares back, clearly not understanding the disdain conferred by Zephyr.

"Well, Luna... there are many things you will need to learn, if you are to succeed in your occupation here, which I am sure you will... if you know what's good for you." The small girl manages to nervously nod her head, not wanting to seem out of place, but granted, this is all she knows and all she will ever know. "The official title of your occupation, as I imagine Onyx may have alluded to you is 'Sorter'. It is one of the most important jobs here in the Upperworld. And failure to properly deliver would have magnanimous repercussions of unthinkable proportions. It is not something to be taken lightly. Have I made myself clear?" Luna glances at Onyx with pleading, fearful eyes, her emotions clearly running on overdrive. But he merely glances back at her with forced calmness,

14

hoping that she won't see past his less-than-authentic facade. "Yes, of course." Zephyr seems to be somewhat satisfied by this, and so he nods and smiles a toothy grin of pristine white porcelain that was likely meant to be encouraging, but had quite the opposite effect.

"Onyx, there are many things I must attend to. Can I have your word that our new recruit will be instructed in the utmost manner, to do the job that she is intended to do, without any repercussions of unthinkable proportions?" Onyx confidently nods, clearly no longer fazed by Zephyr's less-than-welcoming general vibe. "Yes, of course, my leader. You have my solemn promise." Zephyr seems quite pleased with that, and slowly nods. "Authority granted. I release Luna into your domain of tutorship. Teach her well, my servant. Stay true to your task, remain focused at all times. The time has come... to bring her... to the Sorting Room."

CHAPTER 4

"Onyx... where are we going? Slow down!" Onyx slows his pace for a moment, but his hand was still tightly gripped around her own smaller, delicate one. "Little one, you are about to learn the secret of the universe... the purpose of your existence, your ever-present job in this realm. The Sorting Room is where it all happens, and you must promise me that you will listen and learn well. If you don't... well, I wouldn't be able to live with myself..." Luna is clearly taken aback by such a statement, but her ever-growing curiosity was beginning to take over. "Yes, I'll do the best I can. I won't let you down." Onyx strokes a stray dark hair away from her violet eyes, while framing her chin with his strong hand. "I certainly hope you're right about that."

Onyx leads her out of the grand hall where Zephyr resides, and back into the ever-stretching purple horizon of the realm. He continues to drag her along, with urgency, as if trying to meet a certain time-sensitive deadline. Or maybe he was just nervous. Regardless of his reason for rushing her, little did Luna know that she was about to learn something important that would change the way she views life forever.

Within a few minutes, Onyx leads her into yet another large, white structure, similar to the grand hall but with much less intricate decorum. It resembled the habitation pod, but it was infinitely larger in size, with a magnanimous presence comparable only to a juggernaut in one's wildest dreams. The sheer level of cleanliness is impeccable - every inch of it gleams as a great green ball of fire and energy in the sky sends rays of light into the very apex of it, providing the energy for it to carry out its various functionalities in the Upperworld.

"This, Luna, is the outside of the Sorting Room. This is where you will report for work whenever you are summoned on your implanted microchip. If you'll follow me this way we'll enter and begin your training..." Luna can barely keep her eyes off of the incredible scenery she was witnessing. The large, pristinely white, double doors opened up at the touch of their wrists at the security sensor.

"And this, Luna, is the inside of the Sorting Room, the inner sanctum of the realm, and really, of humanity as a whole..." Luna barely hears him finish that sentence - she is utterly wrapped up in the even more incredible experience of the Sorting Room. The Room itself is less like a room, and more like a warehouse running in all directions, seemingly for infinity. The outside of the Sorting Room does not appear to be able to physically hold all the many machines and smooth white capsules arranged in neat rows all over the space. But somehow, it does, because they are all functioning operationally, with many different lights blinking spontaneously, and the corresponding orderlies jumping to their aid. Luna couldn't speak, but not for lack of ability - she was merely caught up in the sheer amazement of the moment.

"What goes on in here? What am I supposed to do? What's my job?" Onyx smiles broadly at her enthusiasm. "Well, aren't you excited! Slow down - I'll explain everything to you momentarily. Or rather, I'd like to introduce you to Jade, the Head Sorter. Luna, this is Jade."

Jade turns to see Luna and suddenly, a shocked expression leaps onto her face, but only for a mere second before she quickly conceals it into one of her well-practiced smiles. *Onyx... is... guiding HER?* But Jade quickly composes herself before her surprised expression is registered by either Onyx or Luna.

Luna turns sharply to her left to meet Jade, the tall, boisterous leader of the Sorters. "Hello! Luna is it? I am Jade, and I oversee everything that goes on in this room. Granted, I cannot accomplish it on my own, but that's where you, and all the other Sorters come in."

Jade was only slightly more personable than the terrifying Zephyr, but Luna felt instantly more at-ease upon meeting her anyway. She has garish, long, silver hair which is tied up into a complex, braided bun, in direct contrast with her rich, dark brown eyes. Jade stands resolute, next to Onyx, as if preparing for an important mission, with her calloused hands staunchly perched on her muscular hips.

"Together, Onyx and I are going to teach you the mechanics of Sorting, and also of the vast importance of your job." Onyx nods his head in accord with Jade. "That's right. My position of Primary Guide means that I am well-versed in every job in the Upperworld. I have studied every aspect of humanoid life, from their psychology to their physiological mechanics and how the two overlap. Literally, every facet of their life is familiar to me, except of course, for the sheer experience of living on Earth. I've never been there, and given the chance there is almost nothing that would compel me to live there. Regardless of my opinions of human life, sorting is likely the most important of them all, as it affects all of that. So it is best that you learn from an expert. In this case, that would be Jade." Jade rolls her eyes. "This guy never stops with the flattery! Anyway, there is much to learn… let's get moving!" With that, Jade grabs Luna forcefully by the elbow, and begins to drag her along, with much urgency, while Onyx follows behind them. One thing that Luna begins to realize in this realm, is that nearly everything is accomplished rapidly… and yet there seems to be no room for error. However, will she manage to thrive here?

"All right Luna. I want you to take a good look around this room and tell me what you see." Luna nods and begins to fully take in the scene unfolding before her. "Well, there are many, many rows of clear, plastic tubes… and glowing stuff sucked down into them." "Good, yes", Jade briskly affirms. "And there are large screens on the walls, with moving images on them. What are those even for?" Jade shakes her head. "Keep observing. I'll explain in a minute." "Well…" Luna begins to be completely caught up in the curiosity and the suspense that she is fighting against so desperately. "Um, there are some small, transparent, glowing orbs that they are carefully placing into the various plastic tubes..." Jade smiles knowingly. "Yes, indeed there are. Any idea what those are?" Luna shakes her head, while Onyx and Jade share a knowing glance.

"Those, my dear...", Onyx begins, "are humanoid souls in their purest form."

CHAPTER 5

Luna's jaw falls open, her bright violet eyes shimmering with renewed amazement and simultaneous fear. "What... what are you doing with them? What are they? Is it painful?" Onyx shakes his head. "Luna, we're not doing anything *to* them. Really, it may be more accurate to discuss what we do *for* them." Jade nods her head. "Absolutely. What we do here, is we decide, based on impulses implanted in us by Zephyr, what life they lead, who they meet, how they live, and basically everything about who they are, through what family they are born into. A Sorter has to learn how to properly fine-tune their gut feelings into a confident decision. Sometimes, the spirit orbs will even slightly glow when held over their life portal." In response to Luna's confused expression, Onyx clarifies some of Jade's advanced terminology for her.

"The 'life portals' are those clear tubes that you had noticed before, Luna. And the 'spirit orbs' are the essence of life on Earth. They are the vessels which carry a human spirit into existence. Each human spirit is generated by Zephyr. He is the one with the master plan behind them all. However, due to the ever-growing amount of spirit orbs flying through here, Zephyr cannot sort them." Jade nods her head. "That's what we're here for. I'm going to demonstrate for you how this works. Watch me carefully. I'll do this a lot slower than usual, just so you can learn. But bear in mind that you'll have to do this at a much more rapid rate than this during the time you are expected to be here working."

Luna nods her head, awaiting her instruction. "Okay, so first, I wait for a fresh orb to roll out of one of the distributor pipes mounted on the wall. Go ahead - touch it, if you like." Luna takes the very tip of her tiniest finger, and makes contact with the unknown surface of the orb. It feels wet, with a slightly cold after-effect. "Uh, okay, it's ummm... kind of slimy." Jade nods. "Yes, that would be the transportation lubricant throughout our tube system. Should one get stuck in transport, that would spell disaster." Anyway, there are many of these, but it doesn't matter which one you take from, because nothing matters until you move it over here to one of the tagging stations. I just hold the orb in the center of the laser focus for a minute... and...." Luna watches as various images appear on the screen, with information listed and all sorts of other things, and she did not have the slightest idea of what it could mean.

"What does all that mean?" Luna points to the large screen which lit up directly above the tagging station. "It tells you the inherent characteristics of this spirit. Some things are negated or adjusted through genetics and other varying factors, but all the basics are here. Try to read through it to get an idea of who this orb will be."

Luna stands on her tiptoes to fully grasp the information superimposed on the screen:

HUMANOID
#8983748460384729384021 7778899
4637382
MONIKER: MORIAH ANN WELLS
BIRTH DATE: 2007
DEATH DATE: 2065
GENDER: FEMALE / HETEROSEXUAL
RACE: AFRICAN AMERICAN
ABILITIES: MUSIC, ARCHITECTURE,
ATHLETICS
PROGENY:
#9783637329274957939292020274582
2048574,
#9783637329274957939292020274582
2048575
PARTNER:
#897472920263746292047465811 12
COMRADE:
#8767392028139475927465839372

    "So, what does all that mean?" Luna's mouth is agape, while Luna and Onyx stand behind her, holding the life-to-be in their hands. "That, little one, is the general information of this orb. The basic details of what will take place in this life." Onyx motions to the orb gently nestled in Jade's palm. "That info is imbedded in the orb itself, so that wherever you are meant to launch it, things will go according to plan-" "unless of course, you put it where it isn't supposed to be." Jade interrupts Onyx to make that last point as clear as possible. "That is the most important fact you must understand, Luna. There is always the possibility that disastrous results can happen from a mistake on your part. Disasters involving the overall narrative of humanity. It's not something to be taken lightly. *Ever*."

Luna is very clearly upset at this point, the color drained from her face and her violet eyes wide with fear. She looks to Onyx for comfort, but he stands next to Jade, stone-faced. Her only ally appeared to be siding with the offender.

"Luna, this isn't something to be afraid of - but rather, something to understand and to be precisely sure about every time you implant an orb into a life. You must follow your heart, and over time, it will become much more apparent to you where to put them. It's something that cannot be taught, but must be learned through experience." Onyx appeared to be trying desperately to stay strong, but kept failing miserably, as he clearly wanted to comfort Luna but had to maintain an emotionless facade.

"And now, Luna, I hold the orb in my hand carefully. Breathe. Let your being merge with the orb through physical contact with the palm of your hand. Your high-tech skin is equipped to sense the inner workings of the orb through life sensors embedded in your hand, and it will be made apparent which life this orb must be deposited into." Luna nods her head slowly, still trying to swallow the fear forming a mound in her throat.

"Okay, this is it, now. Luna, the orb has spoken. I'm bringing it to that tube across the room." Luna and

24

Onyx follow Jade across the large room to a tube mounted on the wall, a downward path into cosmic existence. The trek takes a solid hour. Jade cradles the orb carefully in her hand the entire time, while the subtle sheen of its shiny surface glistens in the harsh, sterile lighting of the Sorting Room. "And then I raise my hand, ever so carefully over the life portal it is meant to go in, and -" Luna gasps as the orb is released from Jade's grasp and plunges into the tube she has chosen. Immediately, the orb begins to sparkle momentarily as it rests in the tube, and then it evaporates into a glittering puff of smoke.

"But where did it go?" Onyx and Jade share a knowing glance. "Well, into life, of course. More scientifically speaking, the orb is invisibly implanted into the uterus of the fated mother through the wiring of the navel. And that's how the humanoids are born."

"What? So it just ends up inside someone? That's... crazy... how does that *really*-" "Sh! Look!" Jade's hand on her face was annoying, to say the least, what with all the questions Luna wanted to ask, but she has a good reason. Onyx is pointing to the small screen above the tube where the orb was placed. It had lit up, with pictures flying across the surface. "That, little one, is footage of the humanoid we had just placed. We can monitor them at any time by inputting their identification number into the tagging machine, but the first few moments of their life are displayed whenever they are successfully implanted as planned."

Luna can't take her eyes off the screen. The sheer realization that she had just witnessed the very origin of that being, the puffy, pink, little blonde-haired infant staring back at her was nothing just a moment ago. "But how did it happen so fast? Didn't we just drop the orb into the portal?" Onyx nods his head in understanding. "Well yes, technically. However, we do not operate in time here in the Upperworld. Therefore, in humanoid reality, nine months had passed - that's the typical incubation period for humanoid fetuses." Although Luna likely understood less than half that explanation, she nods her head slowly, feigning confidence while hoping that it would become real to her in time. Before she had time to respond, that infant appeared to be a young toddler, attempting to walk around what appears to be an Earthly dwelling, and some larger hands grasp around her little body right before she falls. She's giggling, a broad toothy smile spreading on her perfect little face. Quickly reading Luna's enraptured expression, Onyx interjects. "Now two years have passed already. That humanoid is a young child at this point." Another few moments pass and the young child grows bigger, carrying a backpack and sitting in a classroom, her blonde hair held in two pigtails. Another moment passes, and the child is an adult in a white dress... and all the while, Luna looks on and is enraptured by the images flashing across the screen.

Jade nudges Onyx and whispers something in his ear. He quickly nods and turns off the screen with a swipe of his hand. "No need to waste any more time watching that humanoid today. Let's move on."

Luna couldn't help but think that was a little abrupt, as she was quite fascinated with the entire process, but she just continues to follow their lead. "What do we do next?" "Well, there is nothing more to show you at this time regarding the Sorting Room, but rather, you should rest and take some time to ponder the importance of what you have learned. Onyx will escort you to your habitation pod - I will see you when you report for your very first shift in a short while. When it is time for you to report, your wrist will glow bright green. Then you are responsible to find your way here. Until then, Luna." And with that, Jade disappears into the hustle and bustle of the Sorting Room.

CHAPTER 6

"Luna, do you have any questions for me? Is there anything else that I may be able to help you with?" Luna shakes her head at Onyx's willingness to help as they walk to her habitation pod. "No, I think that will be all. It's just... a lot to take in. I am feeling very overwhelmed and I'm not really sure what to make of any of this, really." Onyx nods understandingly. "We all feel like that at one point or another. The sensation will pass. Before you know it, you'll be as confident at your job as any of us." "I sure hope so. I am still scared though." Onyx places a comforting hand on her shoulder. "Don't be. I just know you'll be great. You have already demonstrated a level of sensitivity that I don't usually see in many recruits. And I have trained many new recruits over the last few hundred years." Luna tries to smile as if that helped, but it really didn't. She didn't feel any better about it at all.

"Well, here is your habitation pod. If you need me at all, just speak my name into your right wrist - the embedded device will do the rest. And be aware that should it glow green, you *must* answer it. It is imperative that you remember that. Okay?" Luna nods again, but she can't help wondering why everything here is 'of the utmost importance'. Did these people ever take a break? "Um, Jade mentioned something about my shift in the Sorting Room. When is that again?" "Your wrist will glow green, and Jade will summon you from there. You'll know. Do you think you can find your way there okay?"

Luna shakes her head. "No way. Could you bring me there when it's time?" Onyx nods emphatically. "Of course! I would be happy to. Just call me when you are notified that you need to go. I can be here very quickly. Not to worry, Luna. You'll be just fine."

"Well, there's your pod - you know how to let yourself in. I'll see you when it's time for your shift. If you need me anytime before that, please feel free to call me on your device, for any reason at all. Until then, Luna."

Before she knew it, Onyx wrapped her in his strong arms, producing an indescribable feeling of comfort and peace. Luna doesn't yet understand emotions, but she could feel something happening. Likely his kindness was standing out, as it is the only social warmth she's ever known.

Luna opens the door to her dwelling and waves goodbye to Onyx. She settles onto her recharging station and allows the ample blankets and pillows to swallow her whole body, as if she was safe and secure, and nothing could happen to her. And she was - except for the ever-present duty she had to keep the human narrative on course. It was an indescribable terror of utter importance. In her heart, she knows that when she wakes from her much-needed slumber, she would indeed be summoned to the Sorting Room.

✳✳✳

Luna drifts peacefully asleep, but then awakes to a strange pulsating sensation at her wrist. She looks at her right hand, and it is indeed glowing bright green. A little uncertain about what to do, she instinctively squeezes her arm to activate the communication mechanism.

"Uh, hello?" Her frail voice is connected through her device. "Good day, Luna. This is Jade. I am contacting you to ask you to come to the Sorting Room - it is time for your very first shift. May your choices be ever correct, and may your mind be clear and able to focus. I wish you the very best on your first day." And with that, Jade is gone. Luna decides to call Onyx, as she still has no idea how to get back to the Sorting Room. She gently squeezes her own wrist again, hoping he'll pick up.

"Onyx" she speaks into her transistor. Within a minute, she hears his voice coming through the other end. "Luna? Is it time to go?" Out of habit, Luna nods, but then realizes that he can't see her. "Yes it is - Jade just contacted me." Onyx's level breathing from wherever he was offered some relief to her frayed nerves. If he wasn't worried, why should she be? "Okay. I'll be there in just a few minutes. You'll be fine - not to worry." And then the line went dead. Luna was somewhat comforted by his words but also painfully paralyzed with fear. The thought of directly influencing the course of not only one life, but the entirety of human civilization by association was a large weight to bear - a weight that her own very new existence found it difficult to wrap her consciousness around.

Luna didn't have anything to do for the few minutes she was waiting for Onyx to come and lead her to the Sorting Room, so she just paced around her dwelling, trying desperately to distract herself from thinking about the inevitable job she was about to face. The walls of her cushy pink living pod seemed to begin to cave in. The nerves were getting to her - that was becoming quite apparent. Before she knows it, she merely crumbles to the floor, and fluid begins pouring out of her eyes. It is a strong emotion that she'd never experienced before.

Just when she was beginning to really lose her mind in the worry and pain of her obligation, she hears a bell ring. Logically, she assumes that must be Onyx and raises her arm over the security sensor by the door to let him in. Before he can even get a word out, she crumbles back to the floor, her head between her knees, her violet eyes drenched with tears.

"Luna! What happened to you? Why are you crying?" Luna looks up at him through her moist eyes and her puffy pink face. "I don't know what's wrong... I just... got scared... and then my face got all wet. What's crying?" Onyx wastes no time sitting down next to her, his comforting arm around her shoulders, a gentle hand patting her shoulder. "Oh, my dear Luna... crying is just that - it's an emotional response to strong feelings and your eyes produce water. It's a completely normal thing. But why are you crying? Why are you sad?" Luna can't even formulate words to describe how she is feeling. Her throat is closing up, the nerves are taking over.

"Oh no, my wrist is glowing again…" Onyx taps it for her. "Uh, hello?" "Hi Luna, it's Jade. I was just wondering where you are. I contacted you fifteen minutes ago. Is there a reason why you aren't here yet? There are many orbs to be sorted, we need your help…" "Oh, I'm sorry, I… um…" Onyx interrupts her, and starts speaking into her wrist for her. "Jade, Onyx here. Luna, as you know, is a very new recruit, and is in the midst of an emotional episode. I would politely like to request that you please try to manage without her for just a bit. I'm here with her, and I'm going to try to help her reconcile her concerns. It's better for the process that way, anyway - you wouldn't want her to be distracted in the midst of such crucially important work." Jade is silent for a moment, but then responds in a reluctantly courteous manner. "Hmmm… yes, of course. If you feel that is *truly* necessary. Please make haste though. She is needed here at the earliest convenience." "Yes, of course." And Onyx squeezes her wrist to end the call.

"Now, would you like to tell me why you're so scared? There's no reason to be, really. I just want to be able to help you, but I can't do that if you don't tell me what's bothering you." Luna nods her head through the tears, hoping her face doesn't look as gross as it feels.

"I just… I can't make sense of the pressure that's on me. I'm paralyzed by fear and I feel sick inside. I can't do this… can you tell Jade that I can't? That I just can't." Onyx strokes her wet cheek with his soft hand, and for a few minutes, he just sits next to her on the floor in the middle of her habitation pod, letting her cry, as she buries her wet face in his broad shoulder.

After a small eternity of pain and fear erupting in Luna's small, frail body, Onyx releases his embrace. Luna looks up at him with a level of confusion more akin to hurt than lack of understanding. "Would you, stay with me a bit longer?" Her deep violet eyes glowed with a deep fear that seemed to surpass even the best of any and all encouragement.

"Well, you know I can't hold you forever. You'll have to be brave eventually." Luna pouts her lower lip. "Why? Why do I have to?" Onyx brushes a stray hair off of her face. "Because being a Sorter is *your role*. Everyone follows their role. It's your destined job in the Upperworld and you just... have to do it. It's really not as bad as you think. I'm sorry if Jade scared you - I've been meaning to talk to her about being less harsh to our new recruits - you're not the first one to be pretty upset by her antics."

Although I've never seen one be completely debilitated on the floor before. There is a first time for everything, I suppose. It's as if Luna experiences emotions... more powerfully than other recruits.

CHAPTER 7

"So I really have to get up now?" Onyx smiles at her and rubs her back. "Well, if not right now, then perhaps quite soon. Just think: the sooner you get to the Sorting Room, the sooner you'll get used to everything, and you won't be scared anymore. And before you know it, your shift will be over, and you can come back here if you want. So how about we get to it?"

Luna is none too happy about the arrangement, but nods her head slowly, as if testing the idea in her own mind before verbally expressing it out loud. "Wonderful. Let's go." Luna opens the door, and they both exit her habitation pod.

"Okay, so if you'll follow me out of the New Arrivals District, we'll get back onto the main path, and be in the Sorting Room shortly. Do you have any more questions for me while we're walking?" Luna shakes her head. "I really don't want to think about it."

The purple sky was shimmering the way it always does, but Luna found it to be a bit blinding. Even the pleasantly tepid air typical of the Upperworld around Luna had more of a suffocating effect. Something just wasn't feeling right, but she has no idea how to talk to Onyx about it. She can sense something is very, very off. But she has no idea what. And even if she did, what could she possibly do about it?

For some unknown reason even to her, Luna grabs Onyx's hand as they walk - likely as a source of comfort and security, each of her dainty fingers entwined with his. He offers her a gentle squeeze, and her small, frail, pale hand in his larger, stronger one suddenly feels protected and safe.

✳✳✳

"Okay, Luna. Here we are. If you need me at any time, just - " "No!" Luna stops him mid-sentence with a desperate plea and a desperate arm around his waist. "I mean, would you, maybe, if you don't mind... could you please stay with me for a bit while I work? Make sure I do it correctly? I'm still trying to figure out how this works, and I'd feel safer if I wasn't alone. Please?"

Onyx could sense the desperation in her voice, the way her tone has a certain higher-pitched lilt that signals her immediate need without wanting to look pathetic. He knows Luna has already managed to build a successful facade which casts a shadow for her to cower in. The poor girl needs to gain some confidence, and he was set on giving it to her. As much as he wants to baby her and just make every fear disappear into the thin haze of the Sorting Room, he knew that she would have to learn to fly on her own, and his over-abundant presence would only prolong and hamper the necessary process. But for some reason, this was one recruit that he couldn't seem to shake. Usually with a new recruit (as he's trained many in his four hundred years of existence), he sends them off on their merry way shortly after they are settled into their home and all their questions have been answered. Luna was… different somehow. There was something about her that was subconsciously drawing him to her. It was deeply embedded in his spirit, like an old habit that's hard to break. There seemed to be greater powers at work that were causing Luna to cling to him for dear life like an abandoned child, and him to cling right back to her as if she was… something equally as meaningful to him. But unlike every other recruit and every other post he's held in the Upperworld, there was nothing logical about her. The inherently strange hold she had on him made him question everything, and he had to force himself to be careful about clipping her proverbial wings before she even has a chance to fly.

"Well, I really shouldn't - " Luna's puffy lip made him question his resolve. He wanted her to figure things out on her own. It was so obvious that something about her experience just wasn't right. There was something cooking under Luna's dark-as-raven hair that even she likely couldn't even detect. But he breaks his resolve, as the tears she shed earlier proved that she may be an appropriate candidate for further guidance.

"Okay, I will. But just for a bit. I want you to be able to operate autonomously as soon as possible. I can't stay with you forever…"

"What? What do you mean you 'can't stay with me forever'? *You told me* in the utero chamber that you 'won't leave' me. That's my earliest memory of you. Why did you change your mind? Was I not what you thought I was? Did I do something wrong? What's going on, Onyx?"

Onyx scratched his head in clear discomfort. "I... uh... that's what I say to all the new recruits. You were... in pain. Molecular bonding is one of the worst things you'll experience in the Upperworld. I wanted to ease your suffering, and I suppose I should have been more careful before I promised something that I couldn't keep. I'm sorry, Luna."

The hurt in her bright violet eyes is palpable. Onyx feels hurt to see her suffer this way. "Luna, I'll do whatever you need me to. But you must realize that realistically, you'll have to grow beyond my assistance at some point. Only when you don't need me anymore will I leave you. Until then, I'm all yours. Just... try to learn things. Don't let the fear trap you like this. Your job requires a certain level of strength and intuition. Let your essence guide you. What you need is already inside of *you*."

"But Onyx..." "Shush. Just compose yourself. It is high time to face your fear. I'll stay with you for a bit until you get the hang of things, even though it is quite unorthodox."

Luna, though still troubled by Onyx's strained promise and odd reaction, seems pleased with his response. She is still nervous, but manages to dry her tears and heads into the Sorting Room with Onyx by her side.

"Well look who decided to show up. Welcome, Luna." Jade's snide greeting is immediately met with

Onyx's defense. "Jade, go easy on her. She's had... a difficult time adjusting and is still lacking inner confidence." Jade is annoyed at his rebuttal but holds her tongue, as the hierarchy dictates that Onyx is stationed over her. "Alrighty then. We'll take *good care* of her here. On your way, Onyx..." She's basically pushing him out the main entrance when he stops her dead in her tracks. "No, actually, Luna has requested that I stay with her while she's figuring out her job. I'll leave when she's comfortable."

Jade shakes her head. "Oh, but that's quite unheard of. We need her to - " Onyx raises a hand in front of Jade's flapping lips. "She needs what *I say* she needs. I am her guide. And I will assert myself less politely if challenged any further. Have I made myself clear?" Jade scowls back at him, her already plain-jane face becoming even more ghastly with a good measure of disgust thrown in.

"As you wish." She turns abruptly away from them both, likely to manage another area of the Sorting Room.

"Okay, Luna. Let's get you acclimated now. Go on, go get an orb. You can do this." Luna slowly nods, biting her lip to stop the tears before they slide down her face yet again.

Slowly, yet with a clear intent, Luna marches to the opposite side of the Sorting Room, Onyx silently following her, to the distributor pipe. She slowly, yet deliberately, raises her hand under the pipe, until a small, wet, orb makes contact with her skin. The tiny being was yet unmade, unborn, and nearly inexistent, and yet she was immediately compelled by the importance of it all. The life she held in her hand left a lasting impression in her mind, an impression that would not soon be forgotten, no matter how many centuries she lived for.

"Okay, now take it to the tagging station. Let's learn a bit about this being, shall we?" Luna nods, focusing all her attention on not dropping the small creature she held in the palm of her hand. The orb rolls slightly as she walks to the tagging station, and she flinches, trying desperately not to drop the beginnings of this person on the harsh, cruel floor of the Sorting Room. "So I just scan it right here?" Onyx nods. "Yes, exactly like that." Luna looks up at the screen which is suddenly buzzing with life.

HUMANOID:
#10000000000000000000006758498
2847483
MONIKER: EDWARD ALLEN FORESTIER
BIRTH DATE: 1987
DEATH DATE: 2055
GENDER: MALE / HETEROSEXUAL
RACE: EUROPEAN
ABILITIES:
HUNTING, ATHLETICS, DANCING
PROGENY: NONE
PARTNER:
#1000000000000000000008937463
COMRADE:
#10000000000000000000000000758

"And now, is it time for me to sort him?" Onyx nods his head. "Not to worry though - you *can do this*." Luna takes a good look at the tiny orb in her hand, as if staring at it long enough would get it to reveal where it should end up. "How?" Onyx places his hand on her shoulder, an affectionate sign of support and encouragement. "Close your eyes, let the orb speak to you. Let the fibers of your hand merge with the orb barrier. It will be revealed to you. Relax... breathe." Luna does as she is told, and then looks gingerly around the Sorting Room for a sign. And then she notices something.

"Onyx... that tube over there... it's *glowing*. Why is it glowing?" Onyx smiles. "Well, from what I can see... it's not glowing at all." Luna's face looks quite confused and twisted with frustration at this point. "What do you mean? It's obviously glowing... how do you not see it?" "Luna, only the one holding the orb can see where it is supposed to go. The orb is telling you to bring it to that one - that's a very strong signal you've got there. Most Sorters merely notice a slight pulse in the back of their head, or occasionally a sparkle. That glowing, as you say... I've never heard that from someone before." Luna smiles broadly. "Well, go on. Drop it in."

With renewed confidence, Luna brings the orb to the glowing tube and drops it in. It is immediately received, and the screen above it lights up with images of a little boy swaddled in a blue blanket. "Look - there he is!" Onyx is once again pointing to the screen excitedly. "*You* did that, Luna. Congratulations on your first successful sorting!"

CHAPTER 8

"Is that really him?" Luna couldn't stop staring at the being on the screen, the little boy wrapped up in a blanket. She blinks, and he's a toddler holding the hand of a parent, with a little pack on his back. His smile lit up the screen, his eyes twinkling with the energy of a life well-purposed. "I just... I can't believe it. I did it correctly... so I don't have to worry... I *can* do this!"

Onyx nods his head, smiling at Luna and patting her on the back. "I'm so proud of you. And if you said that the tube really did glow as you say it did... you should know... that exhibits real power indeed. You have so much potential, Luna. You will be an important asset to the Sorting Room, I just know it."

Luna cannot contain the smile spreading on her lips - her entire being was filling with glee. "I think... I'm okay now. If you need to go, I think I'll be all right." Onyx is proud of her... more than even he truly knows, but he isn't too quick to leave her side. Primarily, because leaving a new recruit too quickly could incur serious mistakes. In the lowest, most intimate sanctions of his complex mind, he does not leave her too quickly simply because he inexplicably does not *want* to.

"Only if you truly think you are ready. If you need me, just call me on your implanted device anytime." Luna nods her head. "Yes, I think I can handle this." Onyx slowly nods. "Okay. Good luck. Sort wisely." And with that, Onyx leaves the room, hoping with every inch of his mental faculties that Luna would not make any mistakes. He knew that she could handle the responsibility... but would she get caught up in it all?

✳✳✳

As Onyx leaves the room, Luna decides to get to work on her own. She turns to the orb dispenser on the wall, which suddenly becomes all the more ominous now that she is on her own. Luna freezes in the moment, her hand glued to her side, unable to reach out and grab the orb from the receptacle. She stands there, motionless, for a solid few minutes, and is just about to call Onyx back for help when...

"Hello there. Are you okay?" Luna turns around to see a small girl, much like herself, looking at her with kind eyes and a sweet smile. "Well, are you? Okay, that is." Luna shakes herself out of her paralyzed state to verbally respond to this new acquaintance. "Oh, uh, yes, I'm fine. Just a little... hesitant, I guess? It's my first official day in the Sorting Room." The small girl looking back at her nods her head. "Actually, it's my first day too. I'm Delphine." She outstretches a small, frail hand, just like Luna's. Her hair is pale pink, and tied up into a curt pony tail with a delicate white ribbon. "Uh, I think you're supposed to shake it." Luna smiles out of desperation and reaches her hand to Delphine's outstretched one. "Oh, right. I'm still trying to learn all this stuff. It's... hard to grasp everything, when you're new here." Delphine nods emphatically. "Oh my gosh, I feel exactly the same way! When were you created?" "Uh... well, the whole lack of time thing here kind of confuses me. Recently, I suppose." Delphine nods. "Me too, I think. Well, Luna, we're going to figure this out together." Luna smiles. "So, who is your guide?" Delphine thinks for a minute. "Oh yeah, his name is Evander." Luna nods courteously, even though she doesn't know him at all. "Well, I don't think I've met him. But anyway, my guide is Onyx." Delphine doesn't seem to recognize that name either, so the two just stare at each other in silence for a moment, simultaneously trying to figure out why they met and thinking about how lucky they are to have each other.

"Hey, you two slackers over there! Get to work. I know you're both new and all, but there is much to be done. Get to it!" Luna and Delphine snap out of their silent conversation and nervously face Jade who snuck up behind them. "Oh, uh, sorry Jade. We, uh, we just..." "No excuses, newbie! Get to it!" And with that sudden outburst of annoyance, Jade zips past them to the other end of the Sorting Room, in a major huff.

"Well, she's kind of..." "Horrible. Wretched. Banefully idiotic?" Luna blushes at Delphine's fearless lack of tact, but quietly nods anyway. "Well, yeah, pretty much. But yeah, we should definitely get to it. Here goes nothing! Have you sorted one yet, Delphine?" Delphine shakes her head. "Well, not me, per se. My guide, Evander, sorted one and let me watch while he explained the process. But this will be my first ever, and I'm

terrified. If something goes wrong... I'm so scared."
"That's how I felt this morning. Onyx had to nearly drag me out of my habitation pod. But then, when I successfully sorted one with him nearby, I felt better. That's when I told him that he could leave if he wanted to. He was a little hesitant about it, since I was so worried before. But then he left, so I'm on my own, and you caught me in the middle of another meltdown, actually. I'll demonstrate for you again, maybe that'll help?"

Delphine slowly nods, her soft pink hair bouncing at the nape of her neck. Her frail physique had even a more helpless appearance than Luna - somehow, Luna had gotten stronger while Delphine remained weak and worried. In that moment, Luna vowed to help Delphine, no matter what that entailed. Although they were roughly of the same chronological "age", she felt older, wiser, and stronger than her new friend. Her relatively more-experienced status gave Luna hope that she not only could do this, but perhaps help someone else too.

"Okay, so first, I just collect an orb from one of the dispenser tubes on the wall. Look, there's one over here." Luna leads Delphine by her white, clammy palm toward the tube. Then Luna raises her hand to the tube, and an orb lands on it. "Okay, uh, here it is. Honestly, I'm still a little nervous, but I'm better than I was, that's for sure. Now over to the tagging station!" Luna carefully carries the orb to the scanner, and then looks at the screen. See? This is meant to give you an idea of who this person will be."
Delphine nods, reading the block-type lettering display of

"Anna Rose Mickelson". "Yep, Evander definitely covered that already." "Okay great! And then, after glancing at the screen, you close your eyes, take a deep breath - at least, that's what I do - and then, go where the orb leads you." Luna closes her eyes, and when she opens them, a tube receptacle across the aisle is clearly glowing. "See? I'm bringing it right over to this one. And then…" Luna drops the orb into the receptacle. The screen lights up, and a curly-haired little girl is seen being held by her father, a tall, burly man with a long beard. Delphine is enraptured by the magic unfurled on the screen, and stands agape, much like Luna did upon her first introduction to the Sorting Room. A moment later, the little girl is riding a three-wheeled vehicle of sorts, with presumably her mother walking next to her. "Wow… you just…" Luna nods. "Yeah I guess I did. Amazing, isn't it?" Delphine nods. "Well, I guess it's my turn, huh?" "Well, I am sure you'll do just fine. I was scared too, at first. But once you get over that first one, it gets so *much better.* You'll see - just try it."

Delphine's small frame is shaking as she walks over to the orb dispensing tube nearest her, on the wall. She places her hand under it, the wetness of the orb shocking her hand into total care and submission. "Oh, it's very… wet." "Careful, don't let it slip. I bet that wouldn't be a good thing." Delphine nods as Luna hovers her hands around the orb that Delphine holds. "Okay, now tag it…" Delphine scans her orb under the laser beam and waits for the display on the screen which reads:

46

HUMANOID
#1100000000000484759373929337
7772847829
MONIKER: MIRANDA EVELYN GARCIA
BIRTH DATE: 2002
DEATH DATE: 2085
GENDER: FEMALE / HETEROSEXUAL
RACE: LATINO
ABILITIES:
DANCING, SINGING, WRITING
PROGENY:
#1100000000000000050373627382826
26483682826 6
PARTNER:
#11000000004823746392748749 75
9392
COMRADE:
#1100000000000047638563829374 9
7593

"Okay, here goes nothing…" Delphine holds the orb in her hand, awaiting her inner senses to tell her where this life belongs. "But wait, Luna, how do you know where to go? After you close your eyes and wait a bit?" "Well, for me, the right tube glows, really brightly. I can't explain it. Maybe try looking for something like that?" Delphine nods, but still can't find where to put it. There is a certain vicinity that is shimmering in her mind, a glimmering angle of hope that is working its way through her unsure vision. Without a better option in mind, she slowly moves in that direction, with Luna right behind her, nervously awaiting her choice.

"Okay, I'm going to drop it into this one…" Luna nods, not knowing the correct answer any more than Delphine, since she didn't get to physically hold the orb herself. As if in slow motion, Delphine raises her hand over the tube, and can barely breathe as she ever so slightly tilts her small, pasty-white hand, letting the life-yielding orb roll off her hand and into the vast opening of the orb receptor tube that she chose. Luna smiles for a minute, waiting to see the smiling child appear on the screen. But the screen remains blank.

CHAPTER 9

Sirens blare. Red lights shine down everywhere from the ceiling, with Delphine's chosen tube fogging over with a deathly pallor. The entire Sorting Room is silent, like a tomb. The casual chatter of the workers ceases immediately.

"What - what happened?" Delphine asks Luna, barely over a whisper. Luna shakes her head, all the blood draining from her face. "I... I... I'm not sure exactly..."

The two girls clutch each other in the middle of the Sorting Room. The two of them were in the eye of the storm, the pale-haired rosy one crumbling onto the floor in pitiful tears, the raven-haired girl barely standing, her legs quivering, grasping her new friend in a desperate need for comfort and answers.

Onyx runs over to Luna. "Luna, I heard the sirens from nearby. Was there... an accident?" Luna's face was still white and frozen with fear. "I, uh, um, I'm not sure what..." "Luna! I need you to tell me what happened! Did you see something happen?" Onyx spies the fogged-over tube and the blank screen above it. "Oh this is bad, really bad. I should go find Jade. Stay right here." Onyx wasn't mad - but Luna could sense much concern through his frozen expression. Within a minute, Onyx returned with Jade, who was already on her way over to the disturbance. Sirens still blaring, the forsaken tube that Delphine chose is now fogged over and bright red.

"Okay, we have an incorrect orb placement in sector eighty-seven of the Sorting Room", Jade yelled into her communicator. "Yes, I know, Zephyr. I'm taking emergency reboot precautions now. I'll keep you posted." She grasps her arm to end the call, and sets her sights on the two girls in the eye of the storm.

"You need to tell me what happened over here, and *now.*" Jade had found the source of the disturbance, and she was *not* happy. Livid would be a more accurate term. "The longer we wait, the more difficult it is to fix things. I've paused Earth time for now, while we take emergency measures. Otherwise, that child would have been a teenager in *the wrong family* by now!"

Luna could not quite understand what Jade meant - she is still frozen in fear, so she just listens. Delphine is cowering on the floor, whimpering like a lost puppy. Her guide, Evander, was next to her, trying (and failing) to simultaneously listen to Jade and get his charge off of the floor.

"Whoever did this... catastrophe... will need to be sent down to fix it. Pronto. Either admit it yourself or I will pull out the security tape and scorn you myself, while everyone watches you make a terrible fool of yourself. Go on... reveal yourself."

"Down where?" Luna whispered to Onyx. He whispers back: "To Earth, of course. To fix the mistake that has been made." Earth! It couldn't be. Earth? Where the humanoids are? Alone? To fix what? Luna was horrified at the possibility. Delphine, sweet little Delphine,

heard Onyx's whispered answer, and crumbled further onto the floor, clutching Luna's leg even tighter, weeping profusely.

"All right, I'll give you a minute more to reveal yourself while we pull up the orb info." Jade walked toward the offending tube, typed a few things onto the locked screen, and images appeared. On one side, a young girl looking to be about Luna's age sat on a wall with her arms wrapped around a boy while watching the sunset. It was a pleasant scene. On the other side of the screen, the same girl (Luna assumes) is wearing all black, heavy face paint, and screaming while a different boy plays an instrument next to her. There also appears to be a large crowd of people watching and screaming back at them. *This scene looks horrendous*, Luna thinks to herself.

"I'll explain the magnitude of the situation. This, everyone, is humanoid #110000000000000000484759373929337772847829, with the moniker Miranda Evelyn Garcia.

She was assigned to be partnered with humanoid #110000000000000004823746392748749759392, with the moniker of Anthony Mitchell Stevens, to produce progeny humanoid #110000000000000000050376273828264836828266, with the moniker of Bentley Roger Stevens. However, since *one of you* Sorters has blown your responsibility to the *entire* human race, Miranda Evelyn Garcia has ended up partnering with humanoid under the moniker Garth Ignacio Lopez. You can see Miranda with Anthony on the left screen, as Zephyr himself had intended, and you can see Miranda with Garth on the right screen, which is a terrible, terrible, mistake. She was born, quite literally, into the wrong family, and that is a mistake we can never perfectly fix."

At that moment, Delphine nearly throws up on the floor at Luna's feet. Her face is slowly turning from deathly pale to downright green, the sickness of the terrible error eating her from the inside out.

"We can, and we *will*, however, fix the results of this mistake. If we do not, then the wrong progeny will be born, and a chain reaction of mistaken identities and lives will ensue. That is why we *must* get Miranda and Anthony together. Luckily, Anthony is still in the same geographical vicinity as Miranda, but they have never met in this mistaken reality. Earth time has been paused, but we cannot do that for much longer or else the space-time-continuum could be thrown out of place. I'd say we have about seven minutes Earth time before that happens, and that's not very long at all. Step forward *now, mistaken one, or I will find you myself.* Whoever you are, you must go to fix this."

Jade's stare scanned the room for the offending sorter, and her glare stopped on Delphine. For an unknown reason, Luna frees herself from Delphine and steps in front of Jade before she identifies the perpetrator. Delphine figures out before anyone else what Luna plans to do and screams. But Luna steps forward anyway.

"It was me. I did it. Take me."

CHAPTER 10

Onyx's eyes widen with terror. "What? Luna, this was *your* mistake? How is that possible, you were doing so well..." Luna avoids his gaze - it is too painful for her to lie in the face of the one she trusts the most. "I have to go. Tell me what I need to do." Jade glares at her from under her platinum hair and then drags her forcefully toward a chamber not very different from her utero chamber.

"Get in here. I'm going to press this button, and when I do, your ethereal being will be transformed into that of a human, and you'll be transported to Miranda's closest location. You will feel much different there - the only difference is that your implanted communication device will still be present. That is how you will speak to us, and we'll guide you the best we can. I normally wouldn't want to send such a new recruit down, but in this case, we have no choice. This has to be done." "When will I come back? How will I come back?" Jade is busy furiously pressing buttons on the chamber. "When you get them permanently together, for good, you can call us, and we will have you materialize right back here in this chamber. Until then, you will have to take care of yourself on Earth. That means finding nourishment, also. Here is some Earth currency that you can trade for food. Oh, and there is also the possibility that you might die while on your mission -" "WHAT?" "Oh not to worry - it's not *too* likely, but you should know about that anyway. You'd just end up in the Underworld, no big deal."

"NOOOOOOO!!!!"

Jade is strapping Luna into the chamber now. "Three minutes until time breaks!", someone yells in the crowd to Jade. "I know, we got her. We'll be fine. Luna, we'll be monitoring you the whole time."

"Luna!" Onyx pushes past Jade. "Luna! You did this? How is that possible... your vision is... I can't believe it... I... you're not ready! Jade, she can't go. Unstrap her now!" "Two minutes to go!" that same being yells. Jade nods her head, finishing the process. Before she hits the final button - "WAIT!" Onyx composes himself. "Little one, be brave. Be strong. Be smart. You can do this." "Onyx, I'm scared..." Onyx nods. "I know. But I'll... see you soon. I would come with you, if I could." Luna nods her head, amidst the tears streaming down her face now. "One minute to go!" Jade nods. "I have to do this, Onyx. Move it!"

And then, as the machine hums to life, Onyx inexplicably places his lips on Luna's. He is doing... something. Affectionate, passionate, powerful. Luna feels her body reacting to his embrace, her muscles relaxing, her mouth dancing with his, even though she never learned the steps. It is powerful, and strong, and rushes chemicals into her brain. He pulls away at the last second before the machine responded, breathlessly staring at her in a wide-eyed panic. Luna had no idea what it meant, or why he did that, or why she liked it so much. Onyx seemed surprised too. Her last memory before her body was dissolved by the chamber was Onyx's deep blue eyes wide open, and the other Sorters pulling him away from her with shock and surprise on their faces too. The sensation came to her, and suddenly she was as light as air, a feather on the wind. And then darkness was all there was.

✳✳✳

Luna finds herself lying on a wooden structure under a blue sky, surrounded by green foliage. *Where am I? Oh right... this must be... Earth.* She takes a deep breath, and sits up on the structure. Sitting turned out to be harder than expected. Her body feels inexplicably heavier for some reason, even though she was still herself. Or at least, the Earthly version of herself that she'd never met before. She sits up to look around at her new surroundings... this planet, this world that she'd have to encounter. She looks at the humanoids walking around her, milling about their business. *So these are them... these are the beings that we sort. These are the lives we control, the beings who live out our whims.* Something about the vibe around her feels oddly familiar, an inexplicable deja-vu that she can't explain...

She tries to stand, but immediately feels weighted down again by an unknown force. After a moment or two, Luna stands, and tries to walk. Falling down, she gets up again, fighting the forces that be. *What is this green prickly stuff under me? Earth is so strange. And why is the sky blue? I don't understand this at all.*

Luna is standing in the middle of this green space now, wondering what to do next. She knows that she needs to find Miranda, but has no idea where or how. She barely even remembers what she looks like. Feeling her panicked emotions begin to rise in the back of her throat, she calls Jade on her embedded communicator.

✳✳✳

"Now I'm telling you, Harold, I was walking back to work after my lunch break when I saw this girl materialize right in front of me! No, I swear I'm not drunk. Seriously, I'm not kidding…"

✳✳✳

"Hi, Jade? Um, I'm here, but I'm not sure what to do. Where is Miranda?" "We're watching you on a monitor in the Sorting Room. Miranda is getting ready to play music with her band on that raised structured plateau about fifty paces behind you. Make your way over there and try to talk to her. Befriend her, and earn her trust. Oh, and above all… *never* mention who you really are and where you came from. You'll need to pretend to be a humanoid - so don't let them see you using your communication device. Also, now you are living *in time*. The sun -" "The what? What's a 'sun'" Luna can hear Jade scoffing from the Upperworld through her communicator. "'The sun' is a heavenly body in Earth's solar system which regulates activities and daily activities of the humanoids. It is also their primary time keeper, as Earth's revolutions around it constitute one 'year' as humanoids call it. They also have ages, which refer to their bodily depreciation over time. They are mortal, after all. And for now, Luna, so are you."

At that remark, Luna's breath catches in her throat, this threat of death, an equally unknown and frightening novelty descended upon her. But she pushes it away, as she knows that she should stay focused on the task at hand so she can get home.

"But listen to me - you have to find a place to stay once the sun sets. It is not safe to stay out of doors. And as you are mortal, you will need to sleep, eat, and relieve yourself occasionally. You'll have to figure out that last part on your own. There is much you'll have to learn, because I myself have never experienced any of this. I only know about it through my studies of humanoids. Best of luck to you, Luna. I know you'll be okay. Stay strong, try to find a place to stay for the night if you can." "Uh, okay... I suppose. Jade, can I speak to Onyx? Is he there?" "No, uh, sorry Luna. He's... detained right now. Busy. Attending to... something. Not sure I can say. He'll be in touch with you eventually." And with that, Jade ends the call, leaving Luna's mind spinning.

I suppose I should go talk to Miranda. Jade said she was behind me. Luna turns to look behind her, and sure enough, there is a garishly-dressed girl standing on the raised plateau structure with some sort of a sideways gadget hanging off of her neck with thick strings laying across it. Luna makes her way toward the structure, where it appears that there are other humanoids near her, with similar gadgets and machinery. They are all dressed in very dark clothing with much face paint and eccentricity. Luna feels both curious and frightened by looking at them. Regardless of her feelings, she walks right up to the structure and locks eyes with Miranda, who is a mere eight feet away from her. Luna takes another deep breath and walks up onto the plateaued structure for a little chat with Miranda Evelyn Garcia.

CHAPTER 11

"Zephyr, I'm telling you, there is absolutely *no possible way* that Luna was mistaken. Her orb vision was the most clear I've ever seen in my four hundred years of guiding new recruits. She told me that the correct tube completely *glows* in her mind. No one I have ever met has told me that." Zephyr would not budge on his sure assumption that Luna was the one to blame, but for a moment, his eyes widened at the thought of a glowing tube, but he quickly hid his surprise and remained stone-faced anyway. Regardless of whether or not Onyx was correct in his thinking, his pleas for mercy on Luna's behalf were falling on deaf ears.

"Now, believe me, Onyx. You are one of the best guides we have, if not *the* best. Your new recruit rate of successful assimilation is impressive. It is natural for you to want to defend your own charge - that is understandable. But it does not mean that she can do no wrong. As chronic and disastrous as mistakes can be, once in a green moon, they happen." Onyx was shoving his hands through his pale blond hair, his face red from anger and frustration. "I refuse to believe that she did this..."
"Well, you had told me that she was a nervous one..."
"Well, yes, but most recruits are at least *a little* nervous. If she was not nervous at all, I would be more concerned, as the Sorting Room work requires a vast level of sensitivity and carefulness."

Zephyr nods his head in bland courtesy at Onyx's pleading to bring Luna back home to the Upperworld and to send someone else instead. "Zephyr, I myself volunteer to go if you promise me you will bring her back. She's much too new - she won't last more than a day or two on Earth... I can't let her die. I just... can't." Zephyr could see the pain and anger manifesting in Onyx's eyes, his face tense with agony. "She had... so much promise. She was doing so well, before..."

"Onyx, I understand you are concerned. But I have no choice. The core ruling of our livelihood here is that in the event of a mistaken orb placement, the offending sorter is relegated to fix their mistake in Earthly society as a mortal humanoid. It is dangerous, of course, but that is how we operate. It is clearly detailed in Sector 57, Sub-Section 328 of the Book of Laws."

"But it just... doesn't seem realistic. Do you really think that she can accomplish this? Or survive it at all?" Onyx's blue eyes are moist with desperate tears, a sign of attachment that only Zephyr could explain. Unbeknownst to both Onyx and Luna, there was more to that emotion than what meets the eye, and their tangled emotions hold a deep, dark secret that even they are unaware of. "Regardless of what I think, she needs to be there. You can monitor her on the screen in the Sorting Room, but you should refrain from calling her on her communicator." Onyx's face turned red with anger. "And why shouldn't I?" Zephyr strokes his long, deathly pale chin and his fiery hair seemed to burn stronger momentarily, as it always does when he is deep in thought. "Well, given your recent... ugh... attachment to her, I think you are too emotionally involved with her. In fact, that sort of behavior is a major distraction to our processes here. Do you have any idea how many of our workers are talking about you two? Onyx, you are just lucky that I don't further punish you for posing as such a distraction during such a critical time of damage-control in the Upperworld. You know we cannot encourage physical attraction of any kind - it would distract us from our work." Zephyr tries his best to hide the truth... the reason why Onyx had acted so strange. Zephyr knew exactly why, but has chosen to keep the truth and its evidence locked away deep in the bowels of the Upperworld.

"Honestly... I can't really explain that either. I just... it never occurred to me why I did that. It was... an impulse, I think. I just really don't know. In my four hundred years of existence, I've never felt like this before." Zephyr nods, but his stone-cold expression sucks any meaning out of such a delicate phrase with an undeniably crucial, yet hidden meaning.

"What will happen if I decide to talk to her anyway?" Zephyr's hair begins to burn brighter, as if it is directly linked to his emotional state, and building intensity. "Well, if you do something that defies *me* and my best intentions for *you*, not only will your position of high rank be stripped from you, but you will incur consequences that may cause Luna to struggle... to survive." "Is that a threat?" "Only if you decide it to be."

Onyx takes one last look into Zephyr's cold, maniacal eyes and silently turns on his heel to make his way down the grand hallway and out the door. He had to check the monitor to see Luna's progress. The pain of the possibility of losing her permanently was something he just could not bear. The fear was bearing into his chest, a dull sword poking through all the plans he had for her... all the great things she could have accomplished, down the drain. And the worst thing was - he was still sure that she didn't do this at all. There had to be someone else. And Onyx was determined to find them, bring them to Zephyr, and make *them* be sent to suffer on Earth for this mission. If they were cowardly enough not to admit their fault, then they would pay the price that Luna was unfairly being forced to pay.

✳✳✳

"Hello, uh... Miranda?" Luna looks up at the girl that she was sent to find, who was poised on the raised plateau structure with her instrument strapped to her body. "Yeah? Who's asking?" Luna catches her breath in her throat, trying to plan out every word in order to make her mission go as seamlessly as possible.

"I'm Luna... I uh, came a long way to meet you - "
"Oh, so you're one of those super fans then, aren't you? Well, in that case, I'm pleased to meet you!" Miranda scoots her butt off of the stage and stands next to Luna, her long, dark, curly hair blowing in the wind as the sunlight

catches on her glittery black mini-dress and knee-high black boots. The scent of her garish perfume assaults Luna's nostrils, and she tries not to recoil too obviously. "So, Lana..." "It's Luna..." "Whatever. What do you want me to sign?" "Sign? What? No, that's not what I came for..." Miranda glares back at her, surprised and confused. "Well, then, what can I do for you? I'm not going to give you a free CD, if that's what you're looking for..." "No, I, uh..." Luna was clearly struggling to make progress at this point, so she decided to just play along. "I just... wanted to meet you. I've heard of you... for a long time and wanted to introduce myself. That's all." Miranda smiles. "Oh, okay. Well, thank you for your support. Garth and I really appreciate all our fans. So how long have you been following us?" Luna hesitated, trying to find the right words without giving away her secret. "Well, uh, since the very beginning, I suppose..." Miranda nods. "Well I think that's just great. Oh here's Garth now. 'Hey Babe, can you get over here? We've got ourselves another super fan...'"

A tall, brawny boy around the same age as Miranda appears behind her and also hops off of the raised platform. He has long, dark hair and sports a shabby tee-shirt with well-washed jeans. "Well, hey there, girl. What's your name?" Garth stands next to Luna and puts his hand on her shoulder while tracing a path down to her wrist. "You're a pretty one, aren't you?" Luna looks at him incredulously. "Uh, what?" Garth brushes a hair out of her face. "Yeah, you're gorgeous..." Miranda slaps him hard on his arm. "OUCH! Hey, what was that for?"

Miranda rolls her eyes. "For flirting with a fan. Duh - *so unprofessional.* This is all business, remember? Get back to rehearsal, Babe. I'll be right there." Garth winks at Luna one last time and then climbs back onto the platform to join the rest of the band. "Sorry about that... he's my boyfriend and all... but he's also such a numbskull." Luna really can't understand the phrasing that these two speak, at all. She has never heard colloquial terms like these, as they're never used in the Upperworld. "Well, we're hosting a free concert here in the park in about an hour. Hope you can stay and watch!" And with that, Miranda hops back onto the platform to rejoin Garth and the rest of the band.

Well, that was interesting. Maybe I should come back to the show and watch in a bit. But how long is an "hour"? To answer that question, Luna decides to consult Jade on her communicator. "Jade, are you there? I need to know how long 'an hour' is. How do I measure it?" "Hello Luna. And hour on Earth is a portion of a day, and can be measured by using a clock. A clock is a man-made machine that has a round face and numbers on it. When the arm rotates around in a full circle, that means that an hour has passed. Just look around for one." Luna wasn't totally sure what Jade was referring to, but she tries to look around for it anyway. "Hey, how do you know all this stuff about Earth?" Jade hesitates. "I uh, had to study it... a while ago. Why I did is not important. Anyway, good luck!" "Okay, uh thanks. Bye."

And then, beyond the raised plateau, Luna saw it - a large circular machine in the middle of the green area, with numbers and arms. The arms were both pointing to a "12", so she decided that an hour might be when at least one of the arms goes all the way around the circular face of the clock. *In the meantime, I probably should try to find Anthony. But where is he? I also have no idea what he looks like. Better call Jade again. Or maybe Onyx?*

CHAPTER 12

Onyx is determined to find the real culprit of the sorting mishap. He is still fuming about Luna getting mixed up in all of this. What could have possibly possessed her to admit to a fault that she didn't commit? It was ridiculous, strange, and concerning. He leaves Zephyr's hall and decides to try to call Luna, but realizes that his connection has been cut - he can suddenly no longer use his communicator for any call outside of the Upperworld. But then he remembered Zephyr's threat to strip him of his status if he decides to defy him, and realizes that maybe it is for the best that the temptation is not there. But more than anything, he wanted to, *needed* to, hear her voice, her small, frill, little voice that would reassure him that everything was okay. He wouldn't be able to rest until he knew for sure.

The only thing he could think to do was to march right to the Sorting Room and talk to Jade. She likely saw more of what happened than he did, so maybe she could offer some insight for him.

The walk from his habitation pod was longer than ever - the nagging thoughts and the worries in Onyx's mind, that his protegé, the one he was *supposed to* protect, was out in that cruel, cold, dark world, all alone. And there was nothing he could do about it.

He himself had never been to Earth, but he had heard terribly awful things about it. The way that the entire sky darkens to a pitch black for half the day, and then is resurrected to light by a giant light-filled entity high above. And the people there, their lives are temporary and short. They would be lucky to get a measly 80 years out of the ordeal. The whole thing made his stomach knot and churn. And the worst thing about it all was that now Luna was under the laws of fleeting time, and her own majestic being was relegated to that of a defecating Earth dweller. And that meant, should anything happen to her there, she would be gone forever, doomed to the Underworld. Her mission was likely a fatal one. A mission that she wasn't even close to being ready for - more like a death wish than anything else.

The purple sky is as pleasant as ever, and the air around him is comfortably warm, but it somehow hurt him to see everything around him unharmed by a travesty of such epic proportions.

Onyx enters the Sorting Room to see Jade mindlessly walking around the room, surveying the sorters and wearing that fake smile she always paints on her face as if nothing was wrong at all. The screen to the left was still displaying Luna's live experiences on Earth, slowed down to make sense in the time but not one sorter seemed to notice or even care. They went about their basic business as if nothing at all was amiss. Never mind the fact that Luna was alone, fighting to fix a mistake that she likely didn't even make.

"Jade!" Jade turns to see a very disgruntled Onyx walking toward her. *What does he want me to do? This guide just can't let go of this protegé for some reason.*

68

"Yes, Onyx? What can I do for you?" She paints on her smile yet again, hoping that maybe this time, he would believe it was real. Her smile was the tool she used to keep things calm among the sorters, a magic weapon that enchanted the very thoughts of every single one of them. If she at least *appeared* fine, then the sorters did their jobs successfully. If she disturbed them in any way, more problems could occur.

"I don't think Luna was behind the incident." Jade smiles sheepishly at the nearby sorters who stop what they're doing with a quizzical look on their faces. "Onyx... I'm going to need to ask you to lower your voice. You're disturbing our sorters." Onyx pauses for a moment to control his rising tensions. "Okay... I just... I need to see the security camera footage. I think I can prove this to you. You don't understand..." "Oh I understand just fine, thank you very much. Basically, you are just a guide who has become overly attached to his charge. It happens occasionally - although never for you, I don't think. Regardless, you need to let her go. She'll most likely be just fine. There's nothing you can do - " "Sure there is! I have to clear her name and get her home, here, where it is safe..."

✳✳✳

Delphine is in her habitation pod, shaking. She fled the Sorting Room right after Luna was sent to Earth. The sight of the whole thing was too painful for her to see. And the fact that Luna stepped up to defend her just made things worse.

"Delphine? Are you still in there? There is much work to be done in the Sorting Room..." She rolls her eyes through her tears at the sound of Evander's voice beckoning her outside the walls of her chosen safe-haven. "Yes, I'm here." "Can I come in?" Hesitantly, Delphine raises her wrist to the sensor just as she has been taught, and the door to her dwelling opens with a smooth *hiss.*

"Why are you acting like this? You were doing just fine before, and now you can't even get out of your habitation pod. What happened to you?" Evander stood with his arms folded at his chest, his lips beginning to form a frustrated snarl.

"I... um. I don't want to talk about it." Delphine curled into a ball on the floor and resumed crying. Evander looked on with disappointment in his eyes, his gaze beginning to crowd her thoughts. "Delphine, we've been over this. I need you to be brave. I know that Sorting can be overwhelming, but you were doing just fine. Just because another new girl made a terrible mistake doesn't mean you will - "

That last point did her in. Delphine's sobs turned into uproarious moaning, and her face begin to turn red from the hysteric sobbing. "Evander... I just can't! Please go away... tell them to give me another job to do... I'm not worthy to be a Sorter..."

"Nonsense! You'll gain confidence eventually. You *can* do this. What has gotten into you?"

70

Delphine is silent, except for the rhythmic rocking back and forth on the rug in her dwelling. Beginning to give up hope for a normal conversation, Evander shakes his head, and then gets up to leave.

She wanted to tell him the truth, that *she* was the one that made the mistake, and not him. But she simply couldn't do it. It was all too painful and all too true. The reality of her mistake, and the resulting consequences, were beginning to take their toll on her. The enormous weight that she had to carry on her little shoulders was beginning to dig deep through her neck and muscles, right down into her very essence. The newness of her being could not handle the irascible black blemish on her formerly spotless soul.

CHAPTER 13

Luna is waiting an hour for the concert, but also needs to find Anthony. Without any obvious leads, she calls Jade on her communicator again. "Yes? Luna? What is it now?" Jade was clearly getting frustrated with her at this point. "Uh, I can't find Anthony. Am I close to where he is?" Jade sighs. "Let me check." Luna waits patiently, hoping that Jade will be able to offer some insight into where she can find the boy who is indirectly a part of this mess. She glanced at the large round structure again. The slightly longer arm appears to have moved, but only a little bit. She has plenty of time before the concert.

"Okay, so you're standing in the middle of the green area, right?" Luna nods, but realizes that Jade probably can't see her face. "Yes, I am." "That's the park, so you'll have to cross that street to find Anthony working at the small convenience store counter." "What? I have no idea what you just said. Can you explain it again?" Luna can hear Jade sighing from over the communicator. "Okay, so that area behind you with fast-moving things on it?" "Yes?" "That's a street. And to cross it without getting hit by one of those, you'll have to stand at the end of the white lines painted on the ground, and then walk on those to cross it when the vehicles see you and stop. Once you do that, walk into the little building and ask for Anthony at the counter. He has curly blonde hair, if that helps you at all."

Luna sighs. "Yeah okay, but... I..." "What?" "Jade, I'm scared." "Well, be brave. You have to. You have no choice. Oh, and don't forget to find a place to stay when the sun goes down... someplace safe for the night. I have no idea where, you just have to ask anyone at all. Good luck with that!" And then Jade ended the call, and that was that.

Luna looks up at the sky around her, awaiting some sort of a sign as to what she should do next. She's fighting back the tears of hurt and frustration in the back of her throat, clearly as a result of Jade's harsh treatment of her in her hour of need. She tries to call Onyx, but he doesn't pick up. *Perhaps he has forgotten about me too - nobody in the* Upperworld *seems to care about me at all anymore.* Right there, in the middle of the large green space, Luna crumbles onto the ground in a heap and begins to cry, her greatest fears coming true. And for the first time ever, Onyx isn't there to wrap his strong arms around her and make her feel safe. And maybe he never will be again.

After all her tears were cried and her mood was stabilized for the time being, Luna stands up, dries her eyes, and makes her way to the pathway across the busy area with all those strange vehicles moving across it. She gingerly steps to the side of the pathway, willing with all of her heart that the frightening machines would take mercy on her frail being and allow her to cross the street unscathed. Like magic, the machines *did* see her, and stopped completely, leaving a path for her to cross. A broad smile of relief spreads across her face, and then she walked across the way, feeling powerful and important for the first time in a while.

Upon entering the convenience store, she looks for Anthony around the store. Although, for the life of her, Luna has no idea what she'll say when she gets there. *Hi, I'm from the Upperworld, and it turns out that your entire life as you know it was a mistake. There's a girl that you are supposed to fall in love with but you don't even know her? Yeah, that'll never work.* As Luna's own thoughts begin to eat away at her morale, she begins to lose sight of the real reason she even walked into that store, but then she quickly remembers that she must complete her mission in order to get home to the Upperworld. It's a necessary struggle, and in her heart, she hoped that she could be brave enough. But she really wasn't too sure that she was.

She immediately spies a nappy-headed boy with dirty-blonde hair, just as Jade had described him to her. His curls dangled loosely onto his forehead, his green eyes focused on whatever task he had to accomplish at the big table he was standing at. Luna forces herself to walk over to him, even though she, as of yet, doesn't have a plan as to how to get him to love Miranda. But she was beginning to figure out a good place to start.

"Hi! Are you Anthony?" The blond-haired boy looks up at her from whatever work he was doing. "Ummmmm… yeah? What can I do for you?" Luna's mouth goes dry for a moment. "Well, uh, there's nothing you can really *do* for me, except tell me… ummm, about this place? I'm from… far away." *He has no idea exactly how far...* Anthony smirked. "Well yeah, I can tell. What are you wearing? Some kind of space age costume? Or is it bubble gum?" He motioned to her pale pink rubbery pants and matching long-sleeved shirt. It was typical attire for the Upperworld, but it didn't take Luna long to realize that it may seem out of place on Earth. "Uh, no." Anthony waited for a further explanation, but when Luna didn't say anything else, he just smirks and shakes his head. "Alright then." He starts to walk away, and that's when Luna jumps into action. "Wait! Um, what I was trying to say... was... can you come with me to the concert across the street? It looks like an enjoyable experience..." Anthony raises an eyebrow and then looks back at her. "Are you asking me out, Bubblegum girl?" Luna tilts her head to the side, not quite understanding this colloquial Earth speak. "Well, out of this building, yes. The park where the band is playing is outside." Anthony smirks again, and then lets out a hearty laugh. "You're funny, Bubblegum. Yeah, alright, I guess. I get off my shift in ten minutes. I'll meet you there."

Luna still can barely understand this strange Earth-boy, but she stands where she is, waiting for him to follow her when he has finished his tasks. "Are you really just going to stand there?" Anthony stands behind the counter, likely counting Earth currency, his green eyes poised on her stationary figure. "Why? Am I in violation of a mandate?" Anthony shakes his head in utter amusement. "You sure are a funny one, Bubblegum. Suit yourself, if that's what you want."

Within the next few minutes, Anthony disappears behind the counter, and then re-emerges with a coat and his cellphone in hand. "All right, I'm ready to go if you are." Luna nods, and then walks briskly out the door of the convenience store, making a beeline for the outdoor stage. "Hey! Wait for me!" Anthony catches up to her, and falls into step next to her. "So, you're a Toxin?" Luna's quizzical gaze clued him in to her need for a further explanation. "Are you a fan of Toxic Exposure?" "What?" Anthony brushes a curl out of his eyes. "Um, the band in the park? They're local, you know. They live right here in Boston." Luna still cannot understand his mode of speech. Her mind whirs, trying to process his words. "Um, let's go see them. They're over there." Anthony shakes his head again, but follows Luna to the center of the large green space anyway.

CHAPTER 14

Jade rolls her eyes and shakes her head, but Onyx's unyielding gaze is relentlessly wearing her down. She was tough, but still a sucker for his giant blue eyes. They had an uncanny ability to disarm her soul and break down her walls, regardless of her centuries of prestige in the Sorting Room.

"Onyx... you're not going to like what you see. And you really should get back to work, there are new recruits to integrate from the utero chambers..." Onyx's sapphire eyes turn a mucky tone of midnight at that remark. "And forget about Luna? Clearing her name and getting her back safely *is* my work. I won't stop looking for clues until she's home!" Jade glares back at him. "NO! You must help the other recruits that you've been assigned to! You've wasted enough time on this measly one - don't leave the rest to their own devices! You *must* continue your work. Luna will be back soon enough..." Onyx shakes his head, and with a moment of wild anger, pulls Jade to his face by the collar of her red rubbery jumpsuit. His breath hits her face like a wall of bricks, her eyes filling with fear and utter bewilderment at his sudden outburst. "No... no... I'll never stop looking for her. I'll never stop protecting her! I will arrange for the new recruits to be guided by someone else until I can resume guidance. I am officially out of commission until my Luna is brought home!"

Jade meets his desperate plea with a sly smirk. "*Your* Luna? Since when does she *belong* to you?" Onyx is silenced, his gaze softening, his cheeks beginning to burn. "I... I don't know what came over me." He lowers Jade to the ground and avoids the inquisitive gaze threatening to read through his carefully-measured facade, his hands trembling with anger over her slim waist. "I... do not know why I said that. Just let me see the videos. I refuse to leave until I see the footage. *Now*."

Jade, understandably frightened by his sudden outburst, begrudgingly leads him to the inner sanctum of the Sorting Room to view the footage of that fateful moment when history was changed forever.

✳✳✳

After giving up on getting Delphine out of her blubbery slump (temporarily, at least), Evander reports to the utero chamber complex to update the records on the new recruits and their chemical compounds from their test tube conceptions. He does this routinely, as measured by every ten trillion utero yields, prompted by the notification on his wrist - his job as Treasurer of the Upperworld. But with such a menial routine task, his thoughts are free to roam even while his hands are at work.

Why is Delphine so upset? Maybe she is just overwhelmed... I have seen that happen before. Some recruits are born with a deficiency of the bravery composition, likely a glitch in the lab procedures. I can

78

ask maintenance about that later. But this... I've never seen a recruit relegated to the floor of their habitation pod for days. It is just really... strange. I am getting worried about her. But this job is important - I must pay attention to my updates on the utero records. Zephyr will be very upset if he does not receive his routine report on time. And with that, Evander resumes his work in the utero complex.

Once he is deep in thought with the record keeping, he is distracted with a distinct buzzing coming from inside his small cubicle. He looks around, and when he can't find the source of such an unpleasant buzzing, rendering him useless in record keeping, he slams his fist on his desk. With such force, the fist on his desk rattles the adjacent bookcase, which causes a book to fall behind his desk and onto the floor. "Ugh, I'm so impractical sometimes." Evander forgoes record keeping for a moment to retrieve the book. When he kneels down under his desk, he notices a small aperture in the floor, which appears to be oddly *glowing.* "What could that be? Is that the source of the buzzing?" As if in answer to Evander's self-interrogation, the aperture blinks, its white light beckoning him to explore it further. Before he knows what he is doing, his pale hand slowly reaches out to the opening, the desperate curiosity driving him forward. His office work long forgotten, his mind follows his hand to the aperture. Even the green blinking of his wrist signaling Zephyr's frustration is ignored by his distracted, curious mind. Driven to the light, Evander makes contact with the aperture. He reaches into it as smoke appears, and he nearly recoils for fear of being poisoned or burnt by a security device of some sort. But even fear cannot stop him. His hand reaches in, grasps a small, fogged-over box, and he stares at it, dumbfounded with questions. Before he can open it, his hand weakens as the rest of his body follows, and then his eyes slowly close in a blissful, sinfully deep sleep.

✷✷✷

Feeling powerful and strong, Onyx enters the main security room of the Sorting Room. Jade clamps her lips into an insulting, smug expression which although likely meant to inhibit Onyx's search for the truth, only advanced it. Onyx had vowed eons ago to never let Jade and her antics get to him - he was Primary Guide after all. Zephyr would not have bestowed that title upon him if he was not deserving of it, and that meant that he had every right to see those videos. Nothing Jade said would change his mind.

"All right, Onyx. I have the recording from the last security breach. I believe this holds the explanation that you *think* you need. But trust me, you *don't* want to see this. It will open up a wormhole of more possible questions, and it answers very few questions, if any at all. Are you sure you *really* want this?"

Onyx glares at her for making his quest for the truth so unnecessarily difficult, and deftly snatches the disk from her calloused hand. "All right, have it your way.

I better leave you alone to watch this. It could get ugly and I don't want to be in the middle of you and another tantrum..." And Jade leaves the room as quickly as she had entered with Onyx behind her a moment ago.

Why wouldn't she want me to see this? What could possibly be more disturbing than what has already happened? With his thoughts swirling, Onyx places the small disk into the hologram projector on the table next to him. There he sees Luna and Delphine standing next to an orb receptor, likely trying to complete a humanoid, as Sorters do many times during their shift. Nothing seems amiss until Delphine places the orb into the receptor tube and it fogs over, with bright red lights filling the room and the security sirens sounding their vengeful screams. "I KNEW IT!!! So Delphine really was the one to blame! So... how did Luna get punished for it then?"

✳✳✳

A nearby nurse overhears Onyx's sudden outburst in the main security room as she walks by. She stops for a moment, and is shocked by what she hears. She quickly runs off to tell her newfound information to her fellow nurses. News spreads quickly in the Upperworld.

✳✳✳

It wasn't long before the hologram recording seemed to answer his rhetorical question, because he sees

81

himself appear on the screen, questioning Luna. Delphine had shrunk away to the side, her cheeks bright red, her eyes enlarged with panic. Luna took one look at Delphine, and Onyx, watching the recording, witnesses the exact moment that the crazy idea entered her head. The thought materialized, was analyzed, and then adopted into her being. There was nothing he could have done; he never knew she would do this. Onyx watches the recording of Luna while inhaling short, quick breaths, when she stepped forward into idiotic admittance - the moment she plunged herself into cosmic terror and an uncertain future. What was once set in stone was abolished, her frail young body forced to journey to Earth and suffer, as a substitute for Delphine.

OH DELPHINE! How could she be so stupid! Why wasn't she trained better? She clearly needed more instruction! Who was her guide? Oh yes, Evander. I think that was his name. I'll have to talk to him next... and get to the bottom of this. I bet he doesn't even know about this travesty! And that little imp thought she wouldn't be found out! Ha! Justice will be served, and Luna will be avenged.

CHAPTER 15

"Anthony, they'll be playing on that raised structure over *there*." Anthony catches up to Luna's rapid pace and glances to where she is pointing. "You mean the stage? You sure are obvious, Bubblegum - I kinda knew that already." Luna has no idea what he means, but manages to smile politely anyway. "Yes. There they are!" Without waiting for Anthony to follow her, Luna runs over to the edge of the stage and looks up at Toxic Exposure.

"What's up everyone? ARE YOU READY TO ROCK?" A small crowd begins to form around the structure as nearby park-goers join the festivity and converge into a slightly dignified mob. They scream an answer to Miranda's query, but she barely seems to care. "I can't hear you! Scream like you mean it!" The crowd erupts as the band launches into their opening song. Miranda turns sharply on her tall studded, stiletto heels and conducts the band members with her theatrical vocal performance.

Luna turns to see that Anthony stands right behind her, his body touching hers from the chaos of the crowd pressing them together. Luna finds it strange that the humanoids seem so controlled by the music, their bodies swaying and their mouths agape at all the same times. They are all relegated into a trance-like state, a mindless state of utter complacency. Clouds begin to form over the stage, a holy cathedral to reverently shelter the ritual of rock and roll. The band, the holy vessels; the audience, the penitent sinners.

She stands in the crowd, motionless, while everyone around her dances and jumps violently. Even Anthony behind her seems to be thoroughly enjoying himself, his body rhythmically swaying to the infectious beat.

"Hey Bubblegum, why aren't you having fun?" Luna turns around to meet Anthony's quizzical gaze, his green eyes gazing at her, a point of social connection in an otherwise anonymous crowd. "This is supposed to be... *fun?* What is 'fun'?" Anthony shakes his head and returns to the erratic dancing of the crowd.

The band is feeding off of the crowd-sourced energy. The music is pulsing through their veins... but Luna stands tall, feeling utterly unaffected by the energy whirling around her. She is utterly distracted by her urgent mission - to fix Delphine's horrid mistake and then be taken home to the Upperworld.

Miranda is writhing around on the stage, her sparkly outfit pulsing with an *otherworldly* energy. She opens her mouth and lets out a guttural scream while Garth is next to her slamming on his guitar and violently thrashing his upper body with the tempo and feel of the music. He also nods in Luna's general direction, and sneers seductively. Luna is unsure, and tries to walk away, but then reminds herself that she must introduce Anthony to Miranda, and she must stay until the end of the show to do so.

Luna looks out on to the horizon and realizes that it is indeed getting dark, just as Jade had predicted, and that means that she would need to find shelter for the night. But where does a person get such shelter?

✳✳✳

After a small eternity of heavy metal torture, Luna breathes a sigh of relief when the band finishes their last song and the crowd begins to dissipate.

"Hey! Miranda!" Luna calls Miranda over to the edge of the stage, and she hobbles over in her sky-high heels, her face moist with sweat and red from screaming. "Hey there, Lena, isn't it?" "Uh, it's Luna..." Miranda ignores her correction. "So how'd you like the show? Totally rad, right?" "Uh yes, it was great. But - I'd like you to meet ... Anthony." Anthony diverts his gaze from the overall landscape to Miranda's sparkly-eyed stare. Their eyes lock for a moment, and Luna fills with hope. It looks like some recognition fills Anthony's face... maybe he is realizing his destined life partner. Maybe things are going to be okay now. Wa*s that it? Is that all I had to do? Can I go home now?* And Anthony reaches to gently touch Miranda's shoulder... takes a deep breath... and...

... flicks off a flying insect.

"Oh you had a bug on you. There you go, I got it." Miranda smiles courteously. "Oh thanks. Those damn horseflies are everywhere this time of year!" Luna hides her face in her hands, her hope shattered by the miscommunication of a fly. Anthony smiles but then is caught up in looking at his cellphone. Luna cannot help but stare at this misfortunate pair, the way that they barely even acknowledged each other, and seem to be two completely different people. *How are they possibly still compatible? Miranda was born into a different family with a stark difference in upbringing. This is impossible!*

"Hey there, beautiful…" Garth interrupts Luna's hopeless internal frustration to assert his neanderthal presence into the sphere of her own self-destructive thought process. "Uh, hi?" "So Luna…" Garth jumps off of the stage and leads her slightly out of earshot from Miranda, his hand firmly grasping her elbow. "So I don't suppose you have a place to stay for the night?" Luna's ears perk up at the prospect of shelter for the imminent dark hours creeping along the skyline, as she remembered Jade's strong warning to find shelter. Even the bench where she regained consciousness seemed to be bathed in the beginnings of a dark evening shadow. If she does not find shelter, then she may forfeit her safety and be at the mercy of the darkness and whatever dwells within it. "Uh, no I don't." A sly smile spreads over his slimy lips. "Perfect. You'll stay with me, then."

CHAPTER 16

Evander awakes on the floor under his desk, the small box still in his hand. His body feels numb, it takes time for him to regroup. It is no longer glowing or emitting vapors, but seems to have a strange sort of gummy condensation on it. He composes himself, and slowly stands up, his legs wobbling from his reclined posture while he was out cold only moments ago.

With much hesitation and concern, he places the mysterious box onto his desk, about five-by-five inches in size. Upon further examination, he realizes that it is likely a tiny bio-freezer. The bolts holding it together appear to be of the same type used in the utero chamber lab where the new arrivals are formed.

But what could possibly be in this box, and what could it be doing in my filing office? Evander manages to shake away some of his questions, but most of them just keep returning, clouding his mind from proper judgement - and so with a screwdriver from his desk, he slowly turns each screw until they are loose enough to be removed - and he opens the box.

The box holds a small document on official stationery, folded into a neat little square with the following information attached:

RETRACTED   HUMANOID
#4583920284851111847593030287563

MONIKER: ONYX DALTON MILLER
RETRACTION DATE: 1790 (REASON: ELECTIVE MATERNAL TERMINATION)

INTENDED BIRTH DATE: 1791

INTENDED DEATH DATE: 1850

INTENDED PARTNER: #468392974985739756288839302B

PROGENY: NULLIFIED - TERMINATION WAS UN-AUTHORIZED

AND ALTERING

RETRACTED HUMANOID #468392974985739756288839302B

MONIKER: LUNA ALISON NELSON
RETRACTION DATE: 1794 (REASON: INTENDED PARTNER NO LONGER IN EXISTENCE)

INTENDED BIRTH DATE: 1795

INTENDED DEATH DATE: 1842

INTENDED PARTNER: #458392028411118475930302B7563

PROGENY: NONE - TERMINATION OF PARTNER

SOLUTION: BOTH WILL REMAIN IN CHAMBERS UNTIL RELEASED AT THE DISCRETION OF THE RULER OF THE UPPERWORLD.

Zephyr

WHAT? So Luna and Onyx were both humanoids at one point? Or, almost? How is that possible? Why are they here, then? Evander's whirling thoughts nearly cloud his vision completely, but it still doesn't take long for him to notice the *real* reason for the cryogenic box.

In the formerly-sealed box, lie two separate, pink, gel-like substances. They are somewhat cognizant of small, under-developed fish, with what looks like a primitive beginning of an eye and nose that are only partially formed. The translucent material seems flesh-like, the surface wet and cold to the touch. The two are held securely in the box, arranged in mirror-image positions - the yin and yang of life itself.

What does this even mean? I am so confused... this is utterly unbelievable! I better go bring the remains to Zephyr. And with that newfound revelation, Evander closes the small box, sealing the paper in it with the mysterious substances, places the small box in his pocket, and leaves his filing office to inquire of Zephyr what this all means. For him right now, for Luna, for Onyx, as well as the entire future of the Upperworld, it is critical that he finds out what this anomaly could mean.

✳✳✳

Onyx is viewing the security footage of *that* fateful day in the Sorting Room with wide eyes, and a stomach full of anger. He ejects the data chip from the holograph machine and bolts out the door of the security office after Jade for further questioning.

"Jade! You mean to tell me that Luna *covered* for someone else's mistake? What would make her do this? Why did she do this? What - what can I do to help her?" Onyx runs his hands through his bleach-blonde hair, his blue eyes vibrant with vengeance. "Delphine *will pay* for this!" Jade is unable to respond immediately, and her silence only infuriates him further.

"Well? Aren't you going to explain this to me? How could you have let this happen on *your* watch?" Onyx's ice blue eyes are burning with anger, nearly searing Jade's stone cold, emotionless face. The two are two opposing powers, their infinite strengths working against one another, fire against rock. Jade remains silent, monitoring her words, to keep *the* secret under wraps, for fear that if she told him the truth, that his world as he knew it would shatter into a thousand pieces.

"Onyx, even if I told you, you would not believe me." Her sneering voice only further fuels the fire burning in his very core. Onyx moves closer to Jade's smug, relentless gaze, until his breath is hitting her face with a forceful dominance of desperation, and his strong arms are poised ever-so-carefully on her tough shoulders.

"*Try me.*"

CHAPTER 17

Delphine is still crumbled on the floor of her habitation pod.

The thoughts... won't stop. I can't. Move. I'm dying. My head hurts. Everything hurts. It should have been me... they should have sent me. I'm a coward. I'm a fake. I'm worthless.

Her head is sinking beneath her heart, her small body breaking apart little by little. The sheer thought of an innocent being sent to Earth in her place is beginning to slowly destroy her. She grabs a knife off of the kitchenette area of her habitation pod.

Maybe this is what I deserve after that. Maybe I was never meant to exist anyway.

Ever so slowly, she raises the knife to her own throat, the cool, crisp metal grazing the surface of her pure skin. She applies pressure, awaiting the warm gush of blood to signal the beginning of the end, but none comes. Her skin appears to be indestructible, an exoskeleton effective in protection against outer threats, but quite useless in protecting her against her own paralyzing thoughts. The sheer inability to end it all only prolongs her pain. She gets off of the floor and lays down on her bed, the lush pillows swallowing her weary body like a soul-hungry demon. Without any other escape from her guilted reality, she presses the sleep aid injector on her wrist communicator and allows the sweet, medicated slumber wash over her until her fears dissipate completely into the blackness of her sedated consciousness, at least for now.

Evander re-enters her habitation pod to check on her on his way to talk to Zephyr about what he found, and finds her unconscious on her bed. "Delphine? Are you all right? What's wrong? Are you asleep? TALK TO ME DELPHINE!" He is beginning to panic, until he sees the blue light blinking just below the pale, thin skin on her inner wrist. *Her sleep aid has been employed - she is only asleep. Of course - we are all immortal here.* His momentary panic subsides until he notices the knife in her outstretched hand.

Did she try to harm herself? I'd better bring her to the psychological infirmary. She is in no shape to be able to do her job, and if I can't get her better soon, I'll be failed as a guide. Zephyr told me that I had to get her working soon to avoid certain repercussions.

"Cosmo, I have a recruit that needs some psychological attention... Yes, she is unfit for the Sorting Room until she is treated properly... Okay, I'll give you the pod number... 593, New Arrivals District, Delphine. She's asleep right now, appeared to employ her self-injecting sleep aid. There is also the curiosity of a knife poised in her hand... I suppose I forgot to mention to her that she is immortal. She's been under a lot of stress adjusting to her existence. Quite strange actually - I've never seen a new recruit be this distraught... I wonder what happened to her, poor thing."

Evander carefully sits next to Delphine's sedated body on her bed. He uncomfortably pats her shoulder, and then checks her neck for her pulse. *It's still there. Slow, deliberately there. If it stops we'll have to reboot her, and then she'd have to start all over. Good thing it's still there.*

"Evander, let us in! Can you open the pod door, please?" Evander hits the small red emergency button under the hidden compartment in the wall, in order to open the vacuum-sealed door of Delphine's pod. "She's over here on her bed." Cosmo and two other orderlies barrel into the door with a sterilized stretcher for Delphine's limp body. "Okay, gently place her here. I'll bring her to the Department of Well-Being, where the sedative will be counteracted so that she wakes up." Evander nods, his solemn face filled with concern. "Evander, do you have any idea what caused this?" Evander starts to shake his head, but then remembers something. "She has been nervous while learning to sort, but I remember that she seemed especially upset after the incident in the Sorting Room. I wonder if she was somehow involved in it?"

Cosmo nods. "Yes, that could be something. I'll conference with the Psychiatric Department and decide how to proceed with her treatment. I'll keep you posted, but until then, you should likely move on to your next charge. Go speak with the Guide Department for another assignment." Evander's eyes suddenly become wide with surprise. "Won't she need me, though?" Cosmo shakes his head. "No, you've done all you can. The psychiatric department will do the rest. Delphine is in good hands. Off you go, now!"

Evander hesitates, looks back at Delphine on the stretcher, and forces himself to move on. He's never had to leave a charge before they feel completely ready. But then he reminds himself that others have it so much worse.

Onyx must be losing his mind worrying about Luna right now. At least my charge is safe and sound and did nothing wrong...

✳✳✳

"Jade, I'm waiting." Jade takes a deep breath, but then decides to just tell him everything. What was the use of keeping it from him anyway? She never understood Zephyr's logic. "I'm warning you, when you find out the truth, it's going to change everything. Your very existence will be different from now on, perhaps more difficult than you ever could have imagined - " "Jade!" Onyx grabs her shoulders and pulls her to his face, his ragged, unsure breathing intensified with the pregnant pause. "Tell me *everything...*"

Jade opens her mouth, but promptly closes it. "Well, it's actually not even me that you have to hear it from. Zephyr should be the one to tell you - it was his idea to keep it from you and I wouldn't want to upset him..." Onyx relaxes his hold on her, but maintains his vengeful gaze.

"Take me to him then." Jade nods solemnly, surrendering herself to his desperate plea. "Okay, let's go." Jade motions for Onyx to follow her out of the main security room and out into the purple, hazy atmosphere of the Upperworld.

✳✳✳

Evander walks briskly through the Sorting Room, on his way to debunk his newest accidental discovery. He was told that he would receive his next recruit assignment shortly, but to get back to work sorting until then, that is, after he solves this mystery. Before he exits the Sorting Room, Evander notices a crowd forming around the monitor which broadcasts a live feed of Luna's mission on Earth in slowed-down terrestrial time. He feels ashamed at his own curiosity, and even more ashamed that Jade has decided to publicize her struggles like this - even though mistakes were made, Luna should not be publicly embarrassed like this. Even Onyx who clearly cares so much about her cannot bear to watch her struggle - it appears that it physically hurts him to see her suffer the way that she is. Or it is too painful to be rendered helpless in fixing this whole problem. So he thinks, anyway. Against his better judgement, he joins the crowd for a brief moment, and quickly notices the source of their interest. Luna appears to be following a boy somewhere, his hand firmly grasping her arm. There are three red warning lights beginning to blink on the side of the monitor.

"Hey, do you know what those are?" A fellow sorter turns to Evander, the question barely formed on his lips before Evander forms a response. "Indeed I do, but I wish I didn't." The sorter who asked him the question appeared to be a recently-emancipated new recruit; Evander could tell by the gleam in his eye of new existence, that he himself knew so well. That and his obvious inexperience were tell-tale signs of a rookie.

"Well?" Evander shakes his head with empathetic emotion. "She's likely going to be attacked by that humanoid." The new recruit's eyes widen. "How?" Evander shifts his gaze. "In a very horrible way, the most destructive possible. It may render her unable to return to the Upperworld at all." "Well then you should try to save her!" Evander's bland, helpless expression met the rookie's hopeful gaze. "Well I can't. No one here can save her... without jeopardizing their own existence." Then Evander exits the Sorting Room to bring his newfound curiosity to Zephyr's attention.

CHAPTER 18

"Garth... it is so kind of you to invite me to your habitation pod for the night." Garth turns to Luna as they walk through the darkening park. "Oh yeah, sure... my *what?*" Luna tilts her head to the side in confusion. "Your habitation pod, where you reside?" Garth raises two bushy eyebrows. "Oh I get it - you're one of those UFO chicks. Okay, um, yes. My *habitation pod.*" Luna nods her head, but finds it strange how Garth's hand remains firmly clenched around her own wrist.

"I just mean, it is kind of you to offer me shelter and protection during the dark hours." Garth nods his head sheepishly, with a knowing grin slithering across his face. "Yeah of course... right this way..."

The dusk sky is purple, rapidly turning pitch black. Clouds are forming over the concert pavilion as it fades into the distance. Stars begin to appear, breaking out of their bonds that the daylight imprisoned them in.

Garth leads Luna into a typical suburban yard... except there is a decaying car parked on the front lawn. He fishes a key out of his deep, saggy pocket - still with one hand. The other is guiding Luna right along beside him, as if to keep her from breaking free. She looks around at the yard - there is a tree with a rubber tire hanging off of it, and a few wooden structures just like the one that she woke up on so many hours ago.

"Alright, make yourself at *home...*" Garth not-so-gently shoves her into the room, where a couch and a TV are stationed. Luna forces a smile, even though something about this is beginning to feel more than a bit... *uncertain*. "Okay, so where will I be able to spend the night? On this structure over here I will likely be *very* comfortable..." Garth shakes his head, and then clenches his sweaty hand even tighter around her wrist. "Follow *me*..." And he leads her down a hallway to a room with a bedraggled bed and clothes strewn all over it.

"Oh, this looks quite... nice too." Luna sits on the edge of the bed, politely sliding the tossed clothes away, purely by instinct. "See you when the light returns!" Garth raises his eyebrows again, but manages to understand her gist.

"Not so fast, babe. I'll be staying in here *too*." Luna does not register concern just yet. Although she finds it strange, she allows him to sit down on the bed next to her. "Oh... okay." "And now..." Garth's words ooze out of his throat like his virus-like presence, and his humid breath assaults her face with a sickening determination. "*I'll* keep you nice and warm... rather, things are about to get good and *hot*..."

✳✳✳

"Zephyr, Jade tells me that there is something that I haven't been told... a secret that affects Luna as well? I am pleading, *please* reveal to me what I don't even know about myself. Four hundred Earth years of existence and it seems that I *still* don't even know who I am. And now Luna... it has to do with her too?"

Zephyr sends a knowing glance to Jade, partially confused, and partially infuriated. His flaming hair glows brighter for a moment, and then dies down to its customary smolder. "Jade, have you revealed too much to Onyx?" Jade nods her head slowly, but is quick to explain herself in the midst of such uncertainty. "Well, yes... but it was important to him to know this. Given the... incident recently, there were many questions that I did not feel qualified to answer. Granted, I know of *some* things, but not all the things. And I did not want to overstep my bounds, Oh High One."

Jade's curtsy was likely meant to be of utter honor and respect, but it had quite the opposite effect in context with her slippery logic.

Zephyr overlooks her less-than-honorable gesture and sighs deeply. "Okay, Onyx. I suppose, given the circumstances, it is time that you know the truth. Please sit." A white marble bench in the corner of the Grand Hall quietly levitates over to where Jade and Onyx stand, and they perch themselves on it with bated breath.

"Onyx... you do understand that all our sorters, as well as guides, and various administrators here in the Upperworld are created through our advanced technological endeavors in our utero lab. Cells are spliced together until we have a thriving zygote, which is then rapidly aged until maturity is reached in our utero chambers." Onyx nods his head. "Yes, of course. I've trained many new recruits and seen the process of gaining existence many times. But how is that related to - "

Zephyr raises his pale white hand to silence Onyx's query. "That's just it. Onyx, neither you, nor Luna, gained existence in this manner." Onyx's eyes widen. "What?" Zephyr nods slowly. "You began existence inside the inner organs of a humanoid, on Earth, through a natural reproductive process." Onyx's face goes blank, and his hands begin to shake. "I... I don't understand..."

"Zephyr!" Evander runs into the Grand Hall where Zephyr is speaking to Onyx and Jade. "I found something... something quite strange, in the floorboards of my record keeping office." Zephyr's usually staunchly emotionless face registers some concern, and also annoyance, as it does under extreme circumstances. "Oh, I'm sorry to interrupt - it's just... I figured this was important..." Zephyr solemnly nods when he sees the small cryogenic box in Evander's hand.

"Actually, your timing is impeccable." Evander heaves a sigh of relief. "Oh, okay. So, uh. What is this thing?" "Evander, please open it." Evander slowly unscrews the last bolt on the outside of the cryogenic box. The top opens with a small *hiss* and then the document and gel-like substances are exposed below it.

"In that box, are the humanoid remains of both Onyx *and* Luna. They were both extracted from their maternal humanoids, in the Earth years 1790 and then 1794, respectively - " "But why? How? What?" Onyx interrupts Zephyr with his tangled emotions, this newfound information causing everything that he thought was real and true to crash down, his whole world changed by a pile of flesh in that cryogenic box.

"Onyx, humanoids have a way of... changing the ideal life courses that I have mapped out for them, some with consequences that affect other beings, such as yourself. In fact, we have a whole sect of underground sorters which have the sole purpose of correcting such mistakes - " "I've never had to change anything... I've never heard of any sorters deviating from the master plan..." "You wouldn't have heard of them, they are kept in secret, Onyx. Even you, being the Primary Guide, would not know about them. It's one of the few loopholes we keep running here in the Upperworld. Without them, we would be completely at the mercy of the humanoids. In fact, Jade is one of our underground sorters. She's known about you being... different... since the day you were activated." Onyx locks eyes with Jade. "You knew? How could you leave me in the dark like this?" Jade opens her mouth to explain, but no words come. "Onyx, Jade was sworn to secrecy. She would not have been permitted to tell you even if she had wanted to." Onyx glares at Jade, and shakes his head in disbelief.

"But I still don't understand. Why wouldn't you just send down sorters like you did Luna?" Onyx's relaxed gaze becomes momentarily exasperated. "Now Onyx, you of all sorters know that sending down a sorter to Earth is a very dangerous prospect... we would lose too many if we sent one down every time things did not go as planned." "I still don't understand how I exist, and why Luna is involved in this, and why she's down there if we had a loophole. Why would you scare her like that? She's suffering for no reason now!"

Jade senses Onyx's temperature rising, his heart pounding faster and angrier than it ever should have. She carefully guides him to sit back down on the bench, out of respect for Zephyr, and his own good.

"Your mother..." Zephyr continues to explain Onyx's unique situation. "She was young, Onyx. She was rendered unable to properly take care of you... and so she terminated your being while you were inside of her..." "What? What does that even mean?" Zephyr pauses for a moment, and exchanges a knowing glance with Jade.

"You would have been dead, Onyx."

CHAPTER 19

"Okay, I suppose we can share..." Luna does not want to appear rude, since it *is* Garth's home and everything. "If you say so..." With one smooth motion, Garth pins her shoulder down to his mattress, her small, innocent body at his mercy, and he knows it. Before she can properly process what is happening, his lips are pressed onto hers, biting her sweet mouth until the tender skin begins to bleed. It was kind of like what Onyx had done to her right before she was sent to Earth, but so much more violent, and painful. And her body was not responding the same way. She is filled with inherent terror, even though she had never been taught the dangers of a strange boy. The metallic taste of her own blood fills her mouth, and the rest of her delicate body tenses.

Behind a closed door, Luna's being is compromised forever, the silence of the outside world and the faraway Upperworld appearing blissfully unaware of her agony. Miranda and Anthony are still out there, unattached from each other, sending everything out of control. And Luna is beginning to worry that she can't do anything about it.

Meanwhile a new receptor tube in the Sorting Room appears, and... it... is... *glowing*.

✳✳✳

Delphine awakes in the psychiatric ward, confused as to where she is. The pristine white walls around her and the spotless bed that she was sleeping on signals some sort of medicinal department. She spies a button on her bed next to her and promptly presses it. A moment later, a nurse appears. "Yes, Delphine. What can I do for you?" Her sparkling brown eyes and pristine nurse's uniform instantly make Delphine feel safe and secure, but many questions still remain. "Uh, I was just wondering what I am doing here? I just woke up." The nurse walks over to look at the medical charts stored in a folder at the foot of Delphine's bed. "Oh my, it appears that you have had a bit of a psychiatric *episode* as of late. You've been brought here for evaluation and treatment. We can't have you alone if you are at risk of self-harm. Even if you are immortal, these things are best looked into."

Oh so they know... Delphine begins to realize that even her innermost thoughts are no longer safe from the prying eyes of the Upperworld and those that control it. That gives her an odd sense of both peace and horror. *I suppose they know what is best for me... I'll just let them do whatever they think is best to treat me.* Delphine nods her head, feeling even a bit better after her internal pep talk. "Is there something I should be doing while I'm here?" The nurse smiles, but shakes her head. "Besides resting and getting stronger, nothing at all. Let me know if there is anything else you think you might need, I'm only a click away." Delphine reads the name tag on the collar of the perky nurse - it reads 'Rosie'. "Okay, thank you... Rosie." She smiles and exits Delphine's infirmary room.

"Haven't you heard? She's the one that caused the fiasco in the Sorting Room!" Rosie turns around to another nurse in the psychiatric infirmary. "Oh really? Delphine?" The other nurse nods. "That's what I heard. She's a troublemaker, that one. She let another new recruit cover for her - Luna." Her outstretched finger in Delphine's general direction fills Rosie with remorse for her patient. "Well, we don't know the whole story. There must have been a good reason..." The other nurse shakes her head. "Well, I think anyone who allows another to take their place in that awful place we know as 'Earth' is a fearful coward. I couldn't live with myself if I allowed that to happen to someone else. That poor girl is suffering now for no reason!"

CHAPTER 20

Onyx's blue eyes widen. "Then… how, why am I here now then? What?"

"You, Onyx, as well as Luna, and many other sorters, unbeknownst to them, are considered to be *Retracted Humanoids*. That means that you were originally a sorted orb, just like the billions and trillions of orbs that we sort every minute here. You were retracted because it wouldn't be fair to simply send you to the Underworld before you've had a chance to live. So, we take the remains, and refurbish them in our utero chambers. Just like that, no one can tell the difference. The leftover remains are then held here for our records, under the floorboards of the Upperworld, where they are *supposed* to be hidden from sight. Clearly, we need to find better places to hide things, since it seems they glow upon impact…"

Zephyr's icy cold glare at Evander chills his very core, but then softens when Zephyr continues to say, "But apparently, the truth ended up coming out on its own. That tends to happen more often than I'd care to admit, regardless of my efforts to keep things under wraps."

Onyx is paralyzed on the white, stone cold bench. The new information flooding his system is enough to make his warm blood run cold, his limbs disobeying the signals sent from his brain. His own body is failing him, just the way it seems his own mother did.

"Onyx? Are you okay?" Jade's well-meaning questioning falls on deaf ears, but he manages to slowly nod, at which point Zephyr continues to explain his origin story.

"So... so what about Luna, now? She's down on Earth, and she didn't even do anything wrong!" Zephyr's hair blazes again, and his eyes dart immediately to Jade. "Jade, what does he mean *she didn't do anything wrong?*" Jade shifts in her seat uncomfortably, avoiding eye contact with the Most High Being. "Ugh, well..." "I don't have time for this, Jade. Tell me now unless you want to join her!" Jade exhales briskly. "Well, it appears that she had covered for another new recruit... according to security footage, Luna was an innocent bystander by the fault of... Delphine." "DELPHINE! That recruit ruined the timeline of Miranda and Anthony! We had to stop time for a whole 7 MINUTES! We almost broke the space time continuum that day... Jade, how could you have let this happen?"

Jade sinks down onto the marble bench, and her breathing intensifies, just as Onyx's did. But now she, unlike him, has reason to be frightened. "I don't know! It just kind of happened. I've never, not in my six hundred years of existence, seen a sorter cover for another. I think maybe it was her human tendencies showing through. As you've said before, the retracted humanoids are not exactly common, but definitely not rare..."

Zephyr's hair is ablaze again, but he slowly softens his gaze after the customary few minutes it takes him to calm down. His forefinger and thumb massage the bridge of his angular nose, the very precipice of his blatant façade. "It's true, that retracted humanoids are fairly common. But not as common as you may expect. Rather, it's rare that anyone knows about them. Usually, they blend right into society here without a second glance. It works out quite well, the majority of the time. That is, in your case, unless there's…"

Onyx returns back to the present, his whirring mind slowed down enough to ask - "unless what? Is that about Luna? I still don't know how she is involved with this…"

Zephyr takes a deep breath and then begins to parcel out the information as if it physically hurt him to explain it. "Onyx, when a humanoid is retracted by its maternal humanoid, it is without the validation of the Sorting Room. Without the validation of the Sorting Room, we are unable to work it into the grand scheme of humanoid existence, and there are suddenly consequences. You see, had you not been aborted, you were to be assigned a partner in life, potentially someone to start a family with and love forever. Onyx nods. "That's logical, I've seen it many times with orbs we have sorted. So, what does this mean for Luna?" Zephyr's characteristic deep grin oozes across his face like a sickly, slimy slug.

"Luna, was the one meant for you." Onyx sits limply on the bench. "Oh, so… that explains…" "Why you have human-like feelings for her? Yes, I suppose that would be sound logic. When humanoids are retracted, the human understanding and processing of emotions is so deeply written into the DNA that it is impossible to break it completely in the utero lab. Therefore, you are stuck loving her, no matter what state you are both in. Partially erased, but not completely. Thus, you were rendered stuck in that perpetual mentality, but you must understand that we can't tolerate such carnal distractions in the Sorting Room... our jobs are much too important for frivolous affairs like that - which is why I won't allow you to contact her on Earth. You are much too important here, Onyx, to allow your job to fall to the wayside merely because of a genetic flaw in your chemical composition..." Onyx's face began to turn red. "You mean to tell me that this was all... everything about me... was a *mistake?*" Zephyr strokes his cold, nearly transparent chin. "I wouldn't say... completely. Partially, perhaps. But don't allow that to upset you, it's fairly common, just not widely known. And I've never seen a case as deep-seeded as your own. Usually, our utero workers can erase at least most of the humanity out of the remains. In your case, it appeared to be much too powerful. Yes, that would be considered a flaw. But the good news is, you can be trained to work past it. In fact, I think it may be helpful to get you into shock treatment until you *forget* all about Luna."

Onyx stands up from the bench now. "Shock treatment! Absolutely not! There's no way I'm going through with that! She needs me now more than ever, I can't, I *won't* forget about her. How will I be able to save her if I forget about her?"

"Oh Onyx…" Zephyr feigned compassion while a few of his orderlies wheel a large screen into the grand hall in front of Onyx and Jade. "I thought you already knew! Luna is as good as gone. She won't be able to come back to the Upperworld. Ever." "What? Why?"

"Take a look at what's happening to her…"

∗∗∗

Delphine awakens from a fitful sleep in the infirmary. She's hurting internally from the harsh realization that everyone knows that she's the one to blame for the incident. It's hard enough to have to live with the guilt that Luna naively sacrificed herself for someone she barely knew, but now even her martyrdom is all for naught. Delphine has to live with the embarrassment and shame, and Luna will likely die a pitiful death for a seemingly heroic act that failed to go as planned (if there was even any plan at all).

With a deep breath, she forces herself to get up from the bone-white sheets of the infirmary bed, even while it's becoming harder to avoid the all-knowing glances of the orderlies who know all about her guilty conscience.

It's probably time I go try to find Evander. Hopefully he'll know what to do. And with that, Delphine heads out to find him.

"Dear, you can't just leave without filling out the appropriate forms and allowing time for a final check up. You had quite an episode there -"

"Look, I know I messed up, okay? It wasn't my fault, I didn't ask her to -"

"No, your sleep aid. You employed the use of your self-injecting sleep aid without needing to sleep, which could potentially signal an imbalance in your mental faculties, and thus render you a danger to the critical processes carried out in the Sorting Room. Beyond your obvious fumble, that is..."

Delphine rolled her eyes and bit her tongue to avoid firing back at the rude orderly. She didn't deserve this kind of treatment. Or worse, maybe she did.

CHAPTER 21

Onyx watches the large screen with horror as Luna's image appears in a real-time broadcast. Then, his whole body begins shivering with horror as he watched Luna be taken over by Garth, her small body being attacked under his bigger, stronger one while she screams out in pain. Onyx knows all too well from his Guide training what this could mean for Luna's fate. This was a moment that would not go unnoticed by Zephyr, as well as any other sorter watching the live feed on the screen in the Sorting Room.

"Wait, so does this mean..." Zephyr solemnly nods. "Luna has been naturally inseminated by that humanoid there." Onyx's head drops to his knees, his whole body crumbling from the pain of losing her. "There, there has to be a way..." "There is none." "There is no way that is really true..." "If you don't believe me, then take a look at the Sorting Room tube receptor sect. There is a new one, for Luna, that has appeared in row 20895736483, column 974639397."

Onyx sobs for a few minutes, while Jade awkwardly pats his back. "Does, does she know?" Onyx's desperate query is quickly answered by Zephyr. "She is temporarily unaware of it, but she soon will be. Her internal transmitter has been shut off and will be dispelled from her body very shortly." Onyx continues to sob heavily, his strong back shaking under the weight of his biggest fear coming true.

"I was… I was supposed to *protect* her. I… I *failed*…" Zephyr exchanges concerned glances with Jade and clears his throat with a mighty growl. "Onyx, what's done is done. Now, please follow procedure as expected and begin work with your next protégé -"

"No."

"Excuse me? What do you mean by 'No'?"

"I mean I can't just move on to the next one. Not with what I know now. I wasn't… meant to be here. I wasn't born here -"

"Onyx, you weren't born *at all*. Didn't you hear? Without our intervention, you would have been banished to the Underworld without even so much as a chance at life. You can't be telling me that's what you would have wanted…"

Onyx's cobalt eyes are tinged with a red rim from crying, his nostrils flaring with rage. "You… I never asked for this. Maybe that is all true, but you've let an innocent, unborn girl go down to Earth without any help or training. Why didn't you just banish her to the Underworld immediately? That's where she'll end up anyway, but you *chose* to let her suffer…"

Zephyr's flaming tendrils begin to burn a bright white while his eyes glow with intense anger. "Well, we did what we did. There is no use discussing it now. Since you know everything now, Onyx, I suggest you choose one of two courses of action."

"And what might those be, *Zephyr*?" The name oozes from his lips with such pain and agony under the extreme circumstances of such a disaster.

"Option one: you continue being a Primary Guide for the new recruits as you were, under the condition that you breathe not a word to anyone about what has been revealed to you."

"You mean the fact that Luna and I were both retracted human spirits?"

"Yes, exactly. Only a select few know about that and I intend to maintain that level of security going forward. So if you promise not to breathe a word of what you know to anyone, then, I can reinstate you and continue business as usual.

"And if I don't?"

Zephyr's eyes begin to glow again with utter rage. "Then that unfortunately brings us to Option two: You would undergo shock treatment to make you forget all about Luna -"

"No! Never!"

"Don't be so quick to say no, Onyx. You could forget about your unfortunate human defect and believe that she never even existed. It would allow you to move forward without the emotional pain and baggage that she caused."

"Absolutely not. She needs me. I have to help her... I'm the only one who can."

Zephyr shakes his head. "No, I need you to stay focused on your work. Basically it boils down to this:

114

either keep your memory of her but continue to move forward and work hard, or fail to do that, and or try to interfere with her, and you tie my hands."

"Meaning?" Onyx leans in a bit closer to Zephyr with all the resolve he could muster.

"Mandatory shock treatment. And believe me, I really don't want to have to do that to you, Onyx. You are one of the best I have. I need you to cooperate, for the good of mankind."

Onyx recoils with the resentment of a wild animal shot. "I see."

"So have you decided?"

Onyx grits his teeth and fights the urge to mutter one of the hundred different colloquial terms he learned in his decades of human life studies.

"Option one."

"Glad to hear that."

CHAPTER 22

The sun breaks through the window of a disheveled room. The curtains are a drab shade of mahogany red, and the carpet is gray with mysterious wall-to-wall stains (at least, the portions of it left uncovered by rotting clothing strewn about). The smell is a mix of unwashed laundry and desperation.

Luna awakens in a disheveled mess, her attacker asleep next to her. Any ordinary girl would have exacted revenge on the one who had taken advantage of them in their own moment of vulnerability. But Luna is no ordinary girl. Luna carefully arose from the bed, found her clothing amidst the bedsheets and the debris, and cleaned herself up the best she could with the running water source she found in an adjacent room. Not wanting to wake up the monster, she crept out of that forsaken house, shaking with post traumatic fear. She is bruised, but not broken. She has been harmed, but not destroyed. There is something in her that is simultaneously so close to breaking, but also stronger than even she knew.

Once out of that house, Luna's legs take her far away from there as fast as she could. It doesn't matter where. She just has to get far, far away from the horrific ordeal she had just been through.

Find Miranda. Find Anthony. Get them back together as soon as possible. Get home.

She repeated those four steps in her mind, over and over again, until they filled her subconscious, distracting her from reliving her traumatic night. The lurching in her stomach is either nerves, or anything, really. She's been through so much. And there was so much more she had yet to do. But she is utterly clueless, awaiting any lead, somehow, somewhere.

And when she realizes that she has nothing to guide her, and that even the steps in her head were substantially out of reach, panic sets in. And then she breaks down and cries.

✳✳✳

"Delphine, your vitals look acceptable enough to be discharged. You will be released to your guide shortly." Delphine turned to look at the orderly standing in the doorway of her infirmary room.

"Uh, okay."

The orderly nods with a perfectly fabricated smile smeared across her face, and then leaves Delphine to gather her things and prepare to get back to the Sorting Room.

"Hello, Delphine. I'm glad you're okay. You gave me quite a scare." Delphine is distracted from her preparations by Evander's calm smile warming her frail back.

"Oh, right. Well, I didn't mean to. All of this... was just becoming too much for me." She opens her mouth to continue speaking, but quickly discovers that she has been scared relatively silent. Evander wastes no time in patting her on the back reassuringly.

"Sorting is no easy job. And it is true that you've had a few more... *setbacks* than is typically expected. But I know things will get better."

"But how do you really know that? I feel doomed to... mess up again." Evander nods his head solemnly. "Well, you can hope with all your might that doesn't happen, because it really, really, *really* hurts many people."

Delphine's face paled in the stark electric lighting. "But... I'm scared anyway." Evander wished there was something he could say to make her feel better, but he was out of inspiration.

"Well then, just do it afraid." That was the best he could do, and now all there was left for him to do was hope that it was enough.

On the way back to her pod for a well-deserved rest and time to refresh, Delphine is quickly intercepted with a very frustrated guide.

"*You... you did this!*" Onyx walks lividly over to where Delphine stood listlessly in the middle of the Upperworld's many pathways. "I'm so... sorry, I -" Onyx's strong hand clamps wordlessly over her trembling mouth, silenced by his strength and affluence.

"I don't want to hear it. You made a critical mistake, Delphine. One that cost many people more than you ever thought possible." He shifts his hold on her to make her see the fire in his otherwise aqua-cerulean irises.

"I cannot even *begin* to describe it to you. *Do not let it happen again."* Her moistening eyes meet his in a stare-down for the ages, a silent appeal for mercy. Lucky for the mistaken sorter, the guide is merciful, even if the half-human soul buried away deep in his core was not. She nods emphatically, and then exhales a sigh of relief once he releases her. His harsh gait told her he meant business. Little did she know how much she had truly cost not only the human world, but the lesser known Onyx Dalton Miller.

Meanwhile, Onyx continues to walk the length of one of the main pathways, until he arrives at the utero chamber complex, to begrudgingly resume his work as a guide for a new sorter. But now that he knows the truth - the whole truth - he's been rattled more than he might care to admit. And being rattled is never a useful attribute when ushering new beings into existence.

The utero chamber operator nods knowingly at Onyx, and then hands him the access card to open the utero chamber housing the bubbling beginnings of his next protege. He looks at the tiny, pink, fleshy, writhing glob in the tube, takes a deep breath, and walks through the portal to prepare the light gathering room for its next occupant.

Please don't make me love you. I can't bear to lose someone again. Not like Luna. Never again.

Volume two:
The plan

CHAPTER 1

Luna begins to steady her breathing under a cloudless morning sky. The dawning of a new day brings hope, and with it, the potential of redemption. The bright yellow sun was rising from the ground, promising hours of glorious daylight. Today could be the day that she completes her quest. Or at least, she hopes it is, since she doesn't want to spend any more time in the dark.

Her stomach rumbles, and Luna thinks it might be nerves, until she remembers what Jade mentioned about trading currency for food. She makes a mental note to get some next time she sees an opportunity for a trade.

Okay, now to continue my mission. There was... a setback. That's all, just a setback. I am okay. I have to be.

From her vantage point at the top of a hill in the park, she can see the convenience store where Anthony works, with a menagerie of people milling around it getting their morning coffee and who knows what else. The only thing she could imagine doing was going to talk to him again, and bring him back to Miranda.

Where's the stage? It was just there before...

This sudden revelation made her mission a bit harder, as she now has no idea where to find Miranda. But at least finding Anthony would be half of the goal. Maybe starting there would give her a sense of what to do next. High on the hope running through her veins, a broken and bruised, but very brave Luna, stands up and begins the trek across the park and the adjacent street to Anthony's corner store. It isn't much, but it's all she has at the moment.

Remembering how the busy intersection works is a life saving-skill Luna has learned in a very short amount of time. She looks across the way, and waits until the signal glows green. Then she quickly leaps across the mysterious white stripes on the ground, hoping she doesn't fall through them. She doesn't notice the curious stares of on-looking strangers, but that is likely for the best.

She enters the enchanted doors which part for her as soon as she gets close. *Even Earth has magic in it...*

Anthony appears to be hard at work, but Luna quickly spies his curly tuft of dirty-blonde hair peeking through the boxes on the shelf. Without any hesitation, she marches right over to him.

"Oh, hey Bubblegum. I see you're back." Luna freezes for a moment but remembers that is the moniker he had attached to her. "My name is Luna." He shrugs his shoulders and tosses a half-hearted glance her way while stocking the shelves. "I know, but I like calling you Bubblegum. It suits you better."

Luna nods politely even though that makes no sense to her whatsoever. "So, um, Anthony? May we speak for a moment?"

Anthony pauses his work and gives her a quizzical glance. "Okay, yeah. What's up?" He crosses his arms and stares into her violet eyes. "Uh, well, I'm looking for... food." Luna mentally chides herself for being needlessly worried, but decides to just see where it takes her. The bigger talk about the soulmate mix-up might not be the best thing to lead with anyway.

"Food? You had to interrupt my unpacking to ask about food?" He chuckles to himself. "It's all around you, silly. Just grab what you want and I'll ring you up at the counter." Luna doesn't understand his terminology (per usual), but nods as if she does in order to maintain her cover. "Okay, thank you."

She then takes the opportunity to take in her surroundings, at which point it becomes quite apparent that, as he promised, there are edible objects all around her. She settles on a box of tin-foil wrapped pastries and a bottle filled with a carbonated green liquid. *I'll ring you up at the counter.* Luna remembers Anthony's instructions and walks to the front of the store where he meets her behind the counter.

"No way! I love lemon-lime soda too. My whole family thinks it's gross but it's still my favorite." Luna forces a smile at his attempt at commonality, even though she is still hopelessly lost, and he has no idea that he's her way out of this mess. Or, at least, half of the way out.

"Okay, so that'll be $8.99 for the soda and the toaster pastries."

Luna has no idea what he means until she recalls what Jade had mentioned about currency while strapping her to the machine that brought her here. Without hesitation, she grabs the whole wad of the mysterious greenish paper from her pocket and hands it to Anthony.

"Woah, this is one-hundred and fifty dollars! I only need $8.99 of it. I'd say I appreciate the tip but this ain't a restaurant, Bubblegum." His joke is met with yet another polite, yet clueless expression on Luna's face. "So, here's most of it back, and your soda and toaster pastries." Luna nods, puts the money back into her pocket, and is about to head out the door, before she realizes that she has bigger problems to attend to. She immediately turns around to talk to Anthony.

"Anthony?" He looks up from the mop he's cleaning the floor with. "Yeah? What now?" Luna walks very close to him before saying the three little words that she hoped would get her on the right path to get him to love the girl he was always meant to.

"Where is Miranda?"

"Miranda who?"

"The girl who stood on the plateau yesterday in the park?"

"Oh... do you mean Miranda Garcia in Toxic Exposure?" Luna's clueless face prompts Anthony to further explain himself.

"The local band that was in the park yesterday... playing music... we went to see them together?"

Luna nods emphatically. "Yes. Where can we find them now?"

"Oh I don't know, they could be anywhere around here. They do a lot of local gigs. Wait, did you say '*we*'?" Luna nods. "But what do you need me for?" *I need you to fall in love with Miranda so I can get home.*

"I just… want you to meet her."

"Well I did yesterday, remember?"

"Again. You should meet her again." Luna is banking on the frequency of their meetings to help the probable outcome of their falling in love. It is an algorithm that she thinks could work, but in reality, nothing about relationships can be calculated like this.

"Uh, well. I can check the band page to see where they're headed today." With that, Luna waits while Anthony becomes quite enthralled by a glowing screen, not completely unlike the billions of screens they have in the Sorting Room. But then she realizes the painful truth that by searching for Miranda, she'd likely have to come face-to-face with Garth again. She begins to hyperventilate at this thought, and as she begins to gag, she can feel a small, slimy object writhing its way up her throat, and it neatly slides though her lips, accompanied by some blood, landing on the palm of her hand. She screams, nearly dropping it, while Anthony rushes to her aid.

"Luna, are you okay? What the heck is that thing you just coughed up? That's so gross. I better take you to the hospital…"

"No!"

Anthony pauses mid-panic. "And why not?"

It takes Luna less than a minute to realize that the faint green light is missing from her wrist, and the mysterious, dark, slimy object in her hand is glowing a dim green but is rapidly fading. She puts the pieces together and struggles to hide her steadily-elevating fear.

For reasons unknown even to her, Luna stashes the wiry, black object in her pocket and tries to steady her breathing.

"I'm fine. Really. Just tell me where Miranda is. And fast."

CHAPTER 2

"You are now gathering light. This is a painful process that should take about a minute. If you need me I'll be right here, but I wouldn't suggest speaking until your vocal faculties are ready. It could slow everything down if you exert yourself."

Onyx runs through his instructions to his newly-formed sorter as if they were on a pre-written script. Granted, he's done this thousands of times since his own origin, but suddenly it seemed so small and unimportant in the shadow of both his own stolen life and Luna's stolen potential. *It's a good thing everyone here is invincible, or else I would have already destroyed that little virus, Delphine.*

He sits next to his protege with all the warmth of a stone-cold pillar, while the frail, nearly-formed body shivers, either from pain or shock. Onyx continues his routine through a clenched jaw.

"Remember to breathe as you tolerate the pain. Almost there, no need to worry." Onyx knows that proper care for vulnerable sorters is key so that they quickly build confidence, but helping someone else seems to be near impossible for Onyx as he himself feels broken.

"Ahhhh… ahhhhh…"

"Yes, yes, you can speak now. Congratulations. Now let me scan your wrist."

The fully-formed sorter complies hesitantly, but Onyx is oblivious to this and grabs his wrist with a death grip. "Your name is River. Now follow me to your habitation pod." Onyx maintains his tight hold on River's wrist and drags him out of the utero chamber to his new home at an alarming speed. The purple sky of the Upperworld zips by as they both run, gleaning curious stares from other sorters and guides.

"Scan your wrist to enter the chamber, rest here until you are called for your first shift.

"But what am I supposed to -"

"Best of luck to you!"

And with that, Onyx shuts the pod door and heads to his own habitation quarters. There was much he had to consider before he is called to orient another sorter. And it is becoming more and more unlikely that he'd be able to properly function as a guide until Luna is home. They told him it was impossible, that she could never return, and his blood boiled when he learned that they remotely expelled her communication device from her body. That was his only lifeline to her, broken forever. And now she was utterly alone, infected by the spawn of a human, and humanity itself was still hanging in the balance due to a mistake that she didn't even commit.

Upon reaching his own habitation pod, Onyx curls up on the floor and cries, very much like Luna did when she learned the ramifications of her job in the Sorting Room. Much time passed until he was able to think clearly.

This isn't... a place I want to be without Luna. I can't continue working properly with her gone, but if I don't, they'll make me forget her forever. And I can't let that happen. I am her sole connection to safety. But safety isn't here. No. I have to go. I'm going to go to Earth to save her and raise her child as my own. And I don't care if I ever come back to this wretched place.

Resolute in his decision, and yet feeling utterly horrified at the ramifications of such a plan as this, Onyx knows this is something he just has to do. If only he could figure out how.

"I don't know how, but I'm coming for you, Luna", he whispers to no one in particular, his already muffled voice snuffed out by the stuffy, tepid air of his pod.

✳✳✳

Delphine has been extremely uneasy since the incident that started this whole unfortunate mess, so going back to the Sorting Room was not high on her list of things she wants to do. She's still terrified that something awful could happen again.

"Evander, I know in my heart that I am not fit to be a sorter." Evander meets her gaze with a serious frown. "I understand how you might *feel* that way in light of... ah, recent events. But you must realize that you were quite literally created to be a sorter. Refusing to fulfill your life's work would not bode well, either for you or for the Upperworld."

"But I might mess up again."

"You can't."

"Of course I could! It happened once before, why couldn't it happen again? I myself could be responsible for the mishaps of the genetic makeup of the entire human race!"

Evander scratches his chin. "Yes, you are right to be concerned. But after such a drastic mistake, I will be re-training you myself. So that you know what to do."

Delphine viciously shakes her head. "You don't understand! That's *not* the problem. I *understand* how it works. But my eyes cannot detect light emanating from an orb or its corresponding receptacle tube!"

Evander's eyes widen in surprise. "Really? Are you positively sure?"

Delphine slowly nods. "I think something is wrong with me... I just... I just can't..."

For one of many times, Delphine begins to cry, her tears flowing rapidly down her face while her throat emits wails of pure frustration and fear.

"Well that, my dear, could be *something* to consider..." Evander wraps a tired arm around Delphine's shivering shoulder while trying to contain his own shock. "I'll have to talk to the... authorities about this, and you'll likely be evaluated for fitness of sortmanship." Delphine's wails grow louder, but she slowly nods and buries herself in Evander's shoulder. Once she calms down, he tucks her calmly into her bed so she can rest. Only after shutting her pod door does he make the call that could mean worse consequences than even Delphine could imagine.

"Jade? My prediction appears to be coming true. The system itself is *breaking down*. I'm going to need to meet with you and Onyx to discuss emergency plans and the next course of action. Also, this is code 141 – Zephyr must not find out. We're going rogue."

CHAPTER 3

"Luna, are you sure you're okay?" Luna nods, even though she's panicking inside. "You, you called me *Luna*." Anthony quizzically nods. "Um, because that's your name, right?" Luna forces a smile. "But I like Bubblegum better." A smile spreads across his lips. "Me too."

He looks into her eyes, and his face grows closer. Her heart beat races, but has the reflexive sense to move away before anything happens.

"Uh, let's go find Miranda." Anthony stops short and blushes a little. "Yes, right. Let's... let's go. I'll tell my manager something's come up and I'll be back soon. It *is* urgent, right?" Luna nods. "Okay, I'll be right back."

Anthony gets up from the spot on the mildewed-tile floor they were both sitting on, and runs to the back room. Meanwhile, Luna wipes the blood off of her face in the tiny convenience store bathroom and makes her way back out to the check-out counter. She also grabs her bag of meager purchases off the floor and follows Anthony out the door.

"So, I'm parked right out back... I'll just pop the address into the navi and we'll be off!" Luna nods, trying desperately to hide her fear and confusion. The bloody, wiry, substance in her pocket touches her leg as a reminder of what feels like her impending doom. To keep her mind off of it, Luna decides to eat some of the food she just bought. She rips open the silvery packages and stuffs the dry, thin pastries into her mouth.

"Looks like they're playing in an auditorium a few towns over, about an hour away. So just sit tight and I'll have us there in a jiffy. Oh, I see you're pretty hungry, eh?" Luna stops mid-bite and returns his eye contact from the passenger seat. "Yes. I am very hungry." Anthony continues driving but maintains their conversation. "You know, those aren't all that nutritious. How about we... grab some dinner after this little mission? If you, you know, want to?"

Luna immediately nods, but a little red flag goes up in her head. Anthony has been all too quick to help her at her every little beck and call, but his motive in unclear. *He's not... like Garth, right? He's not going to... hurt me, right?* Luna's judgment was beginning to scare her, but she looks over at his easy smile and the ease about him, and reminded herself that Garth was concerning at the very start. She chides herself for not getting away from that disgusting guy earlier than she did. But Anthony, she could tell, was different. Miranda is a blessed girl to have her fate tied up with his for eternity. Or, at least, her *intended* fate. Thanks to Delphine, things were nearly irreparable. But Luna is determined to fix it. All of it. *And when I do, I'll be going home to Onyx and I'll live forever with him.*

Her thoughts are immediately interrupted by the sick feeling in her stomach, as the less-than ideal food she just ate begins to mix unfavorably with her stomach acid. She opens her bottle of carbonated liquid to wash it down with, but the bubbles make her feel worse. Her eyes close in response to the pain, and Anthony is too busy talking to no one in particular, to even notice.

"… and that's how I accidentally broke my arm while cleaning the kitchen when I was twelve. So… Bubblegum? Bubblegum? Oh, were you sleeping? I'm sorry -"

"No, I was just… relaxing. I'm fine."

Anthony nods, but Luna can still sense the hint of concern in his eyes. "Well, you sure are quiet. And I just realized I know almost nothing about you, besides that you like toaster pastries and lemon-lime soda. What's your story?"

"My story?"

"Um, yeah? You know, where you're from, what your family's like?"

Luna begins searching her mind for any kind of cover that would get him to believe her cover of being just an ordinary girl.

"Well, I'm not from… here. And my family is… complicated."

Anthony nods. "I totally get it. Families can be a royal pain in the ass but you literally can't live without them, if ya know what I mean."

Luna gazes out her window at the landscape buzzing past her. She had never been in a car before and was intrigued by the workings of such an enchanted vehicle. Ironically, the motion calms her frayed nerves and allows her to breathe more deeply than she had been able to for a while. She also marvels at the way she feels so remarkably… safe. Anthony has this effect on her. Maybe it was loneliness, or the emotional disaster she had become after her terrifying ordeal the night before. But she began to worry that Anthony was getting the wrong idea about her, what with them both spending all this time together. And the scariest thing, was that Luna realized that she is beginning to *like* it.

✳✳✳

"Onyx, I promise you, this is *serious*. It's not that *she* made a mistake. Someone *else* did." Onyx's eyes grow wide as Evander wordlessly points upward in the general direction of where Zephyr resides. "But how can you be sure? Maybe we should run a diagnostic check on her" "Already on it, I sent the lab technicians to her habitation pod. She's more comfortable there." Onyx is still quite shaken from the latest revelation of Luna's unfortunate circumstance, and his mind has been preoccupied with ways to cheat the system and get her home, even when he was supposed to be guiding new recruits.

Jade sits deep in thought, the harsh fluorescent lights of their conference room dancing across her silver hair like a crown of light on a scarecrow. "Evander, do you have *any idea* what this could mean for the entire human race? There could be more sorters who are unqualified for their work… any minute, any second, we could have *another* fiasco!"

Three guides of the Sorting Room sit in silence for what seems like a small eternity, pondering the ramifications of what Delphine's inability could imply.

"Okay, so what do we do with the girl? If she cannot sort, she is useless here." Jade's interjection is met with frustrated glares from both Onyx and Evander, because unlike Jade, they both have very complex emotional tendencies.

"You are *not* going to lay a hand on Delphine. She's already been traumatized enough, Jade." She raises her hands up in defeat. "Well, she cannot just sit around. Everyone here *works* for their keep. What did you have in mind, then?"

Onyx rakes his fingers through his bleach-blonde hair. "Well, she can either learn to be a guide…" "Nonsense! How could she teach others when she herself was not even gifted with proper sight?"

"Or… she could lead the resistance…"

"Resistance? Against what?" Jade's silver hair looks like it was zapped by lightning now, her face glowing with a fatal mix of rage and blood-curdling fear.

"Against the powers that govern the Sorting Room."

Evander and Jade exchange worried glances, likely believing that Onyx's sudden breach of proper respect was a direct product of his loss of Luna to an impossible mission without a return ticket back home. They understand his concern, but his emotions transcended the plane of sadness they themselves were capable of, and that disconnect often makes it hard for them to help Onyx properly adapt.

"Onyx, we understand that you've been through... quite a lot." Evander exchanged a knowing glance with Jade. "But, do you... do you think you want to go get some rest and then reconvene later? I'm sure Jade could grant you a short mental health break..." Jade glares at him, but a muffled scuffle under the table suddenly adjusts her attitude and she begrudgingly nods with a clenched jaw.

Onyx shakes his head but hesitates to directly respond. "I'll be fine. I just... *need* to bring her back. I think... anything like this will have to wait until I get this first *problem* addressed.

"*What?* Onyx, I know you have some sort of human emotion left in you since your... retraction, but..." Onyx's previously neutral expression changes to one of defense. "But *what?*" His face silently warns her to tread lightly on this subject of such critical importance to him.

"The entire human civilization hangs in the balance! If there's a potential that sorters are unable to perform the way we are expecting them to, that *must* be the priority..."

Onyx stares her in the eye while using every ounce of self-control he has to keep his fists settled by his sides.

"Okay, well. If you *must*, conduct a mandatory simulated eye-exam for all sorters. You'll have to do it in shifts, and it will take a while. Not to mention developing the technology to do so. But until Luna is home, *leave me out of it.*

Onyx gets up and leaves the room, and neither Jade nor Evander are totally sure if the chill in the room was his acidic mood, or the automated air regulator being activated again.

CHAPTER 4

Luna and Anthony arrive at the venue where Miranda was allegedly playing. They both get out of the car, but Luna hesitates to move forward, as the realization that Garth is likely in the building hits her again with another wave of nausea. She immediately slumps against the side of the car...

"Woah, Bubblegum, are you sure you're okay? What keeps happening to you? I'm really concerned..." Luna turns away from him as his hand slides thoughtfully to the small of her back, which makes her face heat up and her heart beat faster again. Something was happening inside of her, an unwanted connection that was beginning to really confuse things. She had arrived onto Earth with her objective crystal clear in her mind, even if the logistics of accomplishing it were pretty foggy. Luna quickly shakes off her discomfort and forces a smile at Anthony's friendly face wearing a concerned frown. "I'm going to be fine. Just get me in the building... please."

Anthony helps her to her feet, but remains within a few feet of her as they walk, just in case she feels sick again. The front door of the venue looms ahead of them as the sun reaches its apex and subtly begins its midday descent... the darkness of night was on its way once again.

✳✳✳

Contrary to what she knows is good for her, Delphine has a habit of checking in on Luna's live feed broadcasted by one of the many monitors directly outside of the Sorting Room. Evander explicitly told her to rest up while he tries to resolve her problem of not being able to properly sort humanoid orbs, but the whirring emotions and upsetting details of everything going on keeps her wide awake. Seeing that Luna is at least alive comforts her, but the gut-wrenching realization that she would be unable to return keeps her sick to her stomach, because she knows she herself is the one to blame for it. At the moment, she sees Luna fighting nausea in the parking lot with a boy next to her, who seems concerned.

"Delphine, I *told* you to stay in bed. There are things happening that are far too important and stressful to get yourself overtired. Come on now, I'll walk you to your pod..."

"No, wait. Um, I was just... checking in on Luna. She's... she's okay, right?" Evander pauses, looking for the right words to fully explain what has happened to Luna without further upsetting Delphine.

"Well, yes, she is currently physically alive, but her body has been... tampered with to an extent that she can not return here..."

"How? What do you mean by that, exactly?" Evander scratches his chin and stares off into the distance at nothing in particular. A soft, exasperated sigh escapes from his lips, and then he pats Delphine gingerly on the back. "It's nothing for you to worry about. Back to bed now - you're still so weak."

Delphine opens her mouth to protest, but no words come out. Although she is desperately curious, she knows better than to press the matter anymore. She could sense that, although he could be sometimes unnecessarily cryptic, Evander had her best interests at heart and was likely protecting her from knowledge of a fate much worse than death.

At her habitation pod, Evander tucks her in again in her warm bed, the plush pale pink comforter and pillows forming to her gentle frame perfectly. With the blankets tucked up to her chin, he smiles at her reassuringly and turns to leave.

"Evander?"

He turns around and nods at her in the dimly lit room.

"Am *I* going to be okay? Even though I am not able to sort?"

Evander takes a deep breath, to stall for time before answering her with improper information, for such easily excitable ears.

"I will do *everything* in my power to make sure of it."

Still concerned, but seemingly a bit comforted by that claim, Delphine slowly nods her head and closes her eyes. Evander takes that as his cue to leave, and closes the door to her pod on his way out.

Hopefully what little power I have is good enough. She deserves a better life than this. I'll find something for her. I have to.

***

Onyx is slowly becoming emotionally withdrawn and unstable. His every waking moment is concerned with getting Luna home. He has spent countless hours awake, long after a very stoic shift of guiding new recruits to the Sorting Room, drawing diagrams and making lists without any fruitful results. Onyx acknowledges his own inability to complete his task, but knows that he must keep working, because stopping work would incur consequences worse than a stern rebuke. After another especially draining guide session, Onyx walks over to Evander's habitation pod, hoping that by chance, he happens to be available to talk. A quick press to the digital door notification lets Evander know he has a visitor, with a small blue light illuminated on the inside of the door. After a few moments of desperation, the door opens.

"Oh, Onyx. I wasn't expecting you."

Onyx nods. "Can I come in? I think there are some important matters to attend to."

Evander motions him to enter. "Oh, certainly. I'll contact Jade to join us and -"

"No!"

Onyx's quick reaction made Evander's otherwise relaxed face crinkle with concern.

142

"And why not?"

"Because… the matter I want to speak to you about is likely not something she would endorse… I just need to be heard. It is of critical importance to me and I don't think she has the capacity to… understand me."

Evander slowly settles on his nearby couch. "And you think I do?"

"You are the best option I have." Onyx awaits his response with bated breath, his muscles tensing as he holds in the complex emotions bubbling up inside his being.

"Perhaps… but if you want help with Luna, I honestly just wouldn't know what to say. It's not something I can control… any more than you can."

Onyx nods solemnly. "I agree, it's impossible. I've exhausted all my resources trying to think of something to get her out. I've made lists, I've drawn maps of her approximate location with the data I've collected from the broadcasting systems. And yet, every day, I feel like she is further gone than ever. It's ridiculous, and time consuming, and pitiful. I'm breaking inside. I feel like a failure. And it's all thanks to *your* imbecilic recruit!"

"Okay, I understand that I am responsible for Delphine, and things got out of hand, but I don't think you realize the magnitude of -"

"Oh, believe me, I *know*. I know that what happened should have never happened in the first place. That little miscreant should have owned up to her misstep! It should be *her* down there, suffering, *not* Luna. She must pay for what she's done…"

Evander restrains himself from reacting rashly, the way Onyx had been lately. It was hard, but he usually managed to keep his head calm, even when others around him were not.

"I agree that there should be some consequences for her, but nothing too harsh. She's already suffering from debilitating stress and emotional turmoil, and on top of it all, Delphine appears to be defective. If I cannot find a replacement task for her, then I have no idea what I'll do. She cannot be sent to the Underworld... it would not be fair."

Onyx rolls his eyes. "You mean, like being wrongly banished to Earth?" Evander recoils at the jarring comeback, but nods slowly.

"Onyx, I'm starting to believe that you and I are equally concerned about our charges. Now, we can either fight about who did what, or we can band together and save both of them. What do you think?"

Evander slowly reaches his hand out to Onyx, a shaky, pale white treaty meant to patch up the holes that the space-time continuum, and various human limitations, have blown in their previously rock-solid friendship. With a long sigh, Onyx accepts his hand with his own, and the two begin a long strategy session that would hopefully bring the redemption they so desperately needed. With their two strong minds, there is very little they cannot accomplish.

The two guides sat tirelessly for a long time, wordlessly sketching out more diagrams and possibilities.

No ideas came to mind to properly fix everything. That is, until it did.

"Evander..." Onyx slumps in his chair, his head in his hands for the thirtieth time that day. "I've figured it out... I have a solution, but it's risky."

Evander's eyes light up at the prospect of getting both Luna and Delphine the help they need, within the context of the bigger problem of Miranda and Anthony.

"Risky is far from ideal, but it's the best we've got."

CHAPTER 5

"Anthony, where are they?" Anthony continues looking around the venue. "I don't know, it appears that they've already finished playing and are maybe backstage. Let's go try to find them, if you want?"

Luna nods. "Okay." Then she stays nearby him as they both weave their way through the crowd migrating to the exits after the small concert. "I don't fully know if we're even supposed to be back here, but stay close." In response, Luna feels herself grab his hand for some unknown reason. Maybe it was solidarity, or maybe just the need for security. It was definitely something, and Luna was quickly losing the guard on her heart. It was getting extraordinarily difficult to keep her mind on her objective. She looks at a time-keeping mechanism on the wall. If she remembers correctly, she'd only been on Earth a little over 48 hours, and yet it felt like a lifetime. And she was losing touch with everything she thought she knew.

"Looks like they're in here." Anthony jabs his thumb in the direction of a room marked "green room". Luna takes a deep breath and opens the door.

"Garth literally SHUT UP you're being ridiculous. No one here cares about your idiotic belief about the blue M&M conspiracy!"

"I told you it was real, Miranda! Now stop being such a bitch about it." His hand was rested deliberately on her shoulder, both guiding and forcing her to sit in a nearby chair. Her face is flushed with anger, but she manages to show some restraint.

Anthony clears his throat. "Uh, hello guys. My friend Bubble - ... I mean, Luna, wanted to see you. She's a huge fan of the band, I think." He turns to Luna and whispers: "Er, why did you want to see them again? I can barely remember..." Luna racks her brain for a game plan, but as usual, nothing comes to mind. She is numb with panic both from the importance of her mission, but also at the prospect of being in the same room with Garth again. But then she realized... that might just be the key to everything. The source of her pain and psychological turmoil could be just the thing to get Miranda away from Garth.

"Hi, Miranda, I have to tell you something... important." Miranda locked eyes with Luna. "Oh, um, hi. I remember you from the outdoor show the other day... Lena, is it?"

"It's *Luna*."

"Right, right, what's up? What can I sign for you?" Luna calmly shakes her head.

"No, I need to talk to you... in *private*." Miranda tilts her head to the side, curiosity coursing through her brain.

"Well... okay." She follows Luna out to the hallway for the conversation that could change her life forever.

✳✳✳

"So... you're in Toxic Exposure, right?" Anthony's feeble attempt at small talk with Garth, the greasy behemoth, is cringe-worthy.

"No crap, Sherlock."

"How is that?"

"Pretty dope. The chicks dig the bod, so I get a lot of *action*. Makes the job all worth it." Garth thrusts his hips as if the point needed any more explanation.

Anthony tries to smile politely, but the sheer thought of what *action* meant made him squirm. It didn't take a rocket scientist to realize that this guy was a womanizer, and a dangerous one. Anthony is much too proper to ever think that way - his little sister makes him want to be a better man everyday, because she is so innocent and he's her only protection. He is about to pull out his cell phone to pass the time while the girls are talking, but before he can, the door from the hallway bursts open.

A wordless Miranda marches through it as her fist collides with Garth's nose, and a loud crack fills the room.

✳✳✳

"WE'RE DONE!" Her powerful fist knocked him flat on the floor, likely since he was caught off guard. He recoils and cringes for a moment, and then springs up from the ground and takes a shot at Miranda.

148

"That's NOT how you treat a girl. EVER." Anthony catches Garth's wrist, mere inches before his fist made contact with Miranda's face. His face turns beat red, his jaw clenched in utter rage and embarrassment.

"I will ALWAYS do as I please." He shakes Anthony's grip off of his arm as easily as if it was just a little child's grasp. "And YOU, bitch, are going to pay for that." He pushes Miranda against the wall, as her eyes widen in fear, likely not for the first time.

"I... I told you, we are DONE. Us, and the band. We're DONE." Miranda's lip trembles precariously, as a single chaste tear threatens to trace a path down her cheek.

Anthony slips out the door with Luna in tow. "I'm calling the police, he's hurting her." "But wait, you didn't get to talk to her... I wanted you to meet her." Anthony empathically shakes his head. "Another time, we have to leave *now*. I am not getting mixed up with that nut job again."

"Yes, officer, I'm here at the Regal Throne Auditorium on Elm Street... there's an abusive man hurting a girl... yes, okay. Thank you." He ends the call and breathes a sigh of relief. "Well that was intense." They both get back into Anthony's car and drive away before any repercussions from their actions follow them away.

"So, if you don't mind me asking... what in the world did you tell Miranda to make her snap like that?" Luna's violet eyes darken as she began to panic. She didn't want to concern him with her source of shame and terror, and it was hard enough having to tell Miranda, but it was

149

quickly becoming apparent that this was something that she had to say.

"He... hurt me. Really badly."

"How? What? When?"

"The other day..."

Luna continued on with what details she could remember, tears streaming down her face as she continued. Anthony was in such shock that he stopped the car.

"Luna, I'm taking you to the hospital, you've been assaulted."

"No, you don't have to, please don't -"

"I have to. Just a quick check to make sure you're okay. We're friends, aren't we? You have to trust me."

Luna opens her mouth to protest, but realizes that it might be better just to go along with it. She sits silently in her seat until they arrive. Neither of them says a word until then.

CHAPTER 6

"You want me to go where?" Delphine clutches her covers in shock. Evander and Onyx are talking with her in her habitation pod about the plan they have devised to save both her and Luna from a disastrous fate worse than death.

"To Earth. You don't... belong here without the ability to see the glowing of an orb to its intended receptacle."

Delphine begins hyperventilating. "But that isn't my fault! Am I in trouble?" Onyx and Evander exchange glances. "No, you're not, because we haven't told anyone who would tell Zephyr. If he knew, that would be a problem. But no, it's okay. We figured out how you can fix everything."

"Me?" Delphine points to herself in utter disbelief. "Yes, you, Delphine. We want you to go to Earth to take Luna's place." Delphine shakes her head in confusion.

"I still don't understand. And I'm... I'm so scared." She breaks out in tears, and Evander calmly pats her back, but can do little else to console her. Emotions like sadness are very human, and sorters who are not secretly retracted humanoids have a difficult time expressing that properly.

Onyx nods calmly and continues explaining. "When the... incident... happened in the Sorting Room, you changed the course of fate. By sending Luna to Earth, certain... terrible events... have happened to her, which made it against the regulations of the Upper World to bring her back." Delphine nods, sniffling loudly above the pillow she is tightly clutching to her chest.

"So, we want you to go to Earth to fix the original problem of Miranda and Anthony… and then live there for the rest of your days."

"What? So you're banishing me?" Delphine begins sobbing hysterically now, while Evander tries to rub her back more vigorously, but his attempt at consoling her just makes her more tense.

"No, absolutely not. If anything, we are giving you a chance to live. If Zephyr finds out about your disability, then you'd be sent to the Underworld. We'd like to offer you a chance at life before that happens."

Onyx and Evander take turns trying to explain their plan to Delphine, but they cannot get many words in before she starts crying loudly again, her entire body heaving in agony and terror. After she has cried all the tears she could muster, she is finally quiet enough for them to continue their explanation.

"So… it's really my only chance to live? Go to Earth, get Miranda and Anthony together, and then live as well as I can?"

Onyx nods. "Yes, that's the generic idea that I had." Her gaze turns to Evander.

"But… but… you promised you'd do anything you can to protect me… are you just giving up? Is this it?" Evander shakes his head.

"Oh, my dear, don't you see? I *am* doing everything I can to protect you. This *is* me protecting you.

If I don't do this, you'll be forced to suffer and ultimately be obliterated. I will not let that happen."

Delphine slowly nods. "Okay... but what does this have to do with Luna?" Onyx and Evander exchange glances. "By taking her place, you will be her redemption and correct the mistake you created. You'll get Miranda and Anthony together so that she won't have to. Then, since you will be taking over her mission, she'll be freed up in that aspect to be one step closer to coming home."

"That, wouldn't be enough? What's the next step? When will you get her back? If I'm doing this, then I want to be sure it's... worth it. Both for me, and for her." Onyx solemnly nods.

"I can assure you, that it is. And it will be. The next step involves the... correction of her unfortunate... condition. I have not worked out the logistics of that part, completely, but Evander here..."

"I've been working on some technology to get her back, even with her condition making her exempt from being a sorter in the Upperworld. It's against the rules to have her growing a human fetus inside of her, it's a rare occurrence, of course. Actually, this really has never happened before. Anyway, once she's here... and safe... I can surgically have the offending substance removed from her body and destroyed forever. That's why time is of the essence... if the... fetus... gets too big, and it becomes its own entity before we can get her here, then there won't be anything I can do to help her. And remember, time moves much faster on Earth than it does here, so we have to enact this plan as quickly as possible. Jade has managed to slow down time substantially until the mistake is corrected, but it still moves relatively quickly. But I can't get her back here until we get you properly to Earth and you get in contact with Miranda and Anthony. Then, and only then, I can bring her back."

Delphine slowly nods, realizing how critical this situation has become. She is simultaneously relieved to have a grand purpose, but also terrified of leaving the Upperworld forever - it is all she's ever known.

"Delphine, but just so you are aware... I'm going to lead you to someone on Earth that can help you find your way to Miranda and Anthony. Since this is a rogue operation, I can't enable a monitor to watch you on, but I can talk to you through your embedded communication device in your wrist. At least, until it leaves your body after 24 Earth hours. I'll talk you through everything I can in that time frame."

Evander speaks up for the first time in a while: "I know this must be incredibly difficult to take in... are you all right with this?"

Delphine hesitantly nods, but her face is still flushed with tears. "I'm... okay. I just need to know... when? How long until..."

"Until you are transported to Earth? As soon as the transporter room is left unattended, we'll be getting you in there. I've checked the log schedule in the system, it seems it should be available in about eight Earth hours."

"That's not very long, is it?"

154

"No, it's not."

CHAPTER 7

"Anthony, please stay with me... I'm scared."

"Bubblegum, they won't let me in the exam room because I'm not your family. But I'll be right here when you're done, okay? I'll stay right here. I promise."

Luna takes a deep breath and tries to be brave while an orderly leads her into a sterile room behind another closed door.

Anthony sits in a chair in the waiting room, and notices the time on the clock - 3:30.

"Hi, yes, Sunny Side Kindergarten? I'm going to need to request a home transport for my sister, Felicia Stevens... there's been an emergency, and I'm helping a friend right now... Yes, I'll accept the additional charges. Thank you." Anthony ends the call while clenching his jaw. The extra daycare fee didn't bother him as much as the fact that his sister might think he forgot about her. He'll have to explain it to her later. Or, at least, as much of it as he could to a six-year-old.

After about half an hour of waiting, a sobbing Luna is led from the exam room, carrying a folder of notes, by a kind but concerned nurse.

"Are you the boyfriend?" Anthony looks up from his magazine. "Who? Me? Oh no, I'm just a friend. Is she okay?" The orderly sighs and pats Luna on the back. "Well, if you aren't family I really can't say. But I'm sure she'll fill you in. Best of luck, dear. It's a long journey but

I believe in you." Luna continued sobbing and Anthony just looks at Luna, waiting for answers.

"Bubblegum, what'd the doctor say?" Luna shakes her head and just hands him the folder. He opens it gingerly and tries to remain composed enough not to scare her, but the documents and test results show enough. Maybe just words on paper now, but her condition was one that was going to stay for a solid nine months, and then after that, a lifetime of struggle.

Luna has no true understanding of what was happening, but she could sense something was very, very wrong. Since she is not completely human, her condition would not develop at the same rate as it would for a full-blood humanoid - it would be much faster. In her case, it seemed it was detectable after even one day, perhaps a side-effect of the time discrepancy between the Upperworld and Earth. The doctor believed it's been five weeks - Earth is certainly a strange place indeed.

"Hey, um, congratulations? Maybe you don't want to hear that. This is terrible, I know. I just... I'll help you, okay? You can... stay with me as long as you want. My little sister and I, we don't have a lot but I'll share what we have. Okay? Just breathe. It's going to be okay."

"I don't understand... what happened to me..."

"No one ever truly knows why these things happen... they sometimes just do. I'm so sorry Luna. I truly am." He embraces her in a tight hug, and Luna can feel his muscles relax, but hers did nothing at all. He was different, yet similar to Onyx. Both are caring and selfless, but there wasn't a connection like she felt with Onyx. She comforts herself with this realization, as Anthony was meant for Miranda, and she herself was beginning to worry that maybe she was getting in the way of her own mission. But now she knows.

✳✳✳

As quietly as he can, Onyx straps Delphine to the table in preparation to be zapped to Earth by the molecular scrambler in the small transporter room. His hands nimbly fasten the connectors, rendering Delphine completely vulnerable. But she isn't struggling - no. She has accepted her fate and is ready to start a mortal life on Earth.

Onyx is rattled by the recurring flashback of the day Luna was sent to Earth. He absentmindedly touches his finger to his lip, which now begins to tingle in remembrance of the intimate moment they shared, much to the chagrin and shock of onlookers in that pivotal moment. He himself did not fully understand it, but it shattered his world. He could not, would not, perceive his existence in the same way ever again.

Evander holds her hand. "Delphine, you should know that you will be sorely missed. This... was not how things were meant to go. I wanted... I expected... to get to show you the ropes here, and I thought I'd be working alongside you for eternity. I see now, that will not be the case. But I did want it to. You will be missed, my dear.

Take courage, be brave, and live as happily as you can. I will never forget you."

With a tiny nod filled with pain and dread, Evander slowly nods to Onyx to flip the switch. Delphine's slim frame tenses, then relaxes, and rapidly disappears in a cloud of glittering dust.

Evander's face stiffens, and becomes slightly pale. But he doesn't cry - he just solemnly nods and walks out of the room. But Onyx... Onyx is remembering Luna even more vividly than before. The banishment of Delphine has reopened a barely-healed wound. Now, even more than ever, he is determined to get her back, as quickly and carefully as the last glittering particle floats to the floor.

Onyx leaves the transport room, and follows Evander back to his habitation pod.

"Evander... what are we... what are we going to tell everyone? What are we going to tell Zephyr?" Evander smiles nervously and shakes his head. "Nothing at all. I cannot think of a single thing to say." Onyx hesitantly nods. "Well, we did *technically* find her a new job..." Evander shakes his head. "Even that is classified information. The by-laws state that no one is ever allowed to change occupations in the Upperworld." Onyx nods. "Very true. And the worst of it is... it may imply a defect in the Sorting Room."

Evander leans closer to Onyx. "Do you think she is... a retracted humanoid also?"

Onyx stops in his tracks, slightly offended. "What does *that* have to do with anything?"

"Since she is unable to sense the glow of an orb."

"Irrelevant. Luna and I both can, and we're…" Onyx cannot bring himself to say it. His recent realization about his own origin shook everything he thought he knew to shreds. And being that he holds a position of responsibility and prestige in the Upperworld, it destroyed the confidence he had in himself.

Evander realizes his verbal blunder and pats Onyx apologetically on the back. "I'm… I'm so sorry Onyx. That was very improper of me to say. Well perhaps… there is another reason."

"If we don't figure it out… unqualified sorters could crop up. This could spell disaster!" Evander nods. "I know… we'll… have to think of something."

Little do they know, that their conversation is being listened to. In the shadows of the Upperworld directly outside of the transport room, Jade hears their conundrum and is ready to strike.

"Delphine is gone? Well that's not right… and she was unable to sort? Fascinating." She drums her fingertips mischievously on her chin, willing to break apart everything the guides were working on, as a conniving grin oozes across her lips.

CHAPTER 8

Paralyzed with confusion and worry, Luna forces herself to breathe deeply while she sits in the passenger's seat of Anthony's car. Suddenly they are both at a loss for words.

"So... um... do you like pizza? I know of a great place... I'll call now and order some takeout. I'm sure my sister's hungry too, so we can bring it home and eat." Luna nods, even her minimal amount of words stuck in the back of her throat. *Is this why I lost my embedded communication device? How will I get home? How will anyone help me?*

All these thoughts begin to make her shiver. Her mind is running a mile a minute, and Anthony is oblivious to her internal struggle being more deep and twisted than simply just an unwanted child. *Onyx, will I ever get to see you again? You... you promised...*

"Here it is. I'll... go get it. Just wait here." Anthony stops the car and then carefully opens the door to get the food. It suddenly seems as if her precarious condition subconsciously affects everything he does now - he even appears to walk more carefully than his typical jaunty strut. Within a few moments, he emerges from the building carrying two large, flat cardboard boxes.

"Alrighty, and my house isn't far from here." He inserts the key into the car's ignition, beginning the short trek back to his humble home as the calming, delightful scent of the pizza fills Luna's nostrils. "You know, this is… going to be hard, I know. But I meant what I said earlier about supporting you. You can stay with me and do whatever you need to be comfortable. I'm so sorry this even happened… I wish I knew sooner so I could have helped you more." Luna nods gratefully, but she still clings to the hope that one day, she'll be back home where she belongs, a silent prayer on her lips that Onyx will come to her rescue… and that somehow, Anthony will find his way to Miranda, as Luna is quickly running into a bunch of dead ends.

"This is it." Luna looks up from her silent reverie at a smallish, cozy house that has clearly seen some levels of neglect, with vines marching up the sides of the building and some rogue weeds dotting the lawn substantially. But the glow inside of it is welcoming against the backdrop of the bright purple evening sun.

"My parents… didn't make it after a freak car accident about a year ago." Anthony pauses to look out at the horizon line with a tear threatening to roll down his cheek. "They left everything to us, including the house. And I got custody of Felicia, since I was 18 I can legally be her guardian. It's a lot, for sure. But we're okay. I work a couple jobs, and luckily the mortgage was already paid off so I only have to keep the lights on and the water running. That's the abridged version, anyway. If you were… wondering."

Truth be told, Luna isn't wondering at all, as she is much too wrapped up in her own problems to compare her worries to his. But she senses that he shared something really personal and potentially painful, so she manages a small, unassuming smile as to avoid tipping him off to the magnitude of her internal struggle. It's nearly too much for her to bear, how could she ever expect someone else to?

"Felicia! I'm home!"

A young girl who also bears Anthony's characteristic blond curls jogs in from the back room, making a beeline for Anthony and then hugging him tightly at the waist.

"Anthony!" She looks at Luna for a moment. "Who's the *girl*?" Anthony blushes a shade of bright red, quickly understanding the implications of his sister's innocent mistake.

"She's... uh... a friend that will be staying with us for a while. In fact, why don't you show her to your room? Maybe she can sleep on the other cot."

Felicia smiles brightly. "Okay, come on, girl! Let's go!" She grabs Luna's hand and tugs her excitedly up the small stairwell.

Luna is hardly in the mood for any kind of pleasantries after the day she had, as well as the impending disaster growing inside of her. She feels like a ticking time bomb, hardly able to take care of herself, much less an unwanted human being.

"So, this is your bed." Felicia points to a small cot next to the only window of the small purple room. "And this one's mine!" The little girl starts bouncing on her own bed in glee, clearly happy to have a roommate, blissfully unaware of the difficult circumstances surrounding the arrangement.

"Oh, I almost forgot - I brought home pizza!" Felicia's eyes light up at her brother's announcement. "Yay, that's my favorite!" Anthony beams at his younger sister. "I know. Let's go eat!" Felicia runs out of the room, presumably heading to the kitchen, leaving a silent Luna in the room alone with Anthony.

"I know this isn't ideal, but you really are welcome here. I want you to know that. Please don't worry. I'll figure out a way to explain all this to a six-year-old, just not quite yet. I'll need a little time to figure that part out."

Luna nods understandingly. "I appreciate your generosity. Thank you, Anthony." He nods solemnly. "Well, we better go eat. Felicia may look small but that girl has a huge appetite."

Anthony leads her out of the bedroom and they both join Felicia downstairs in the kitchen.

CHAPTER 9

"Mighty Zephyr, I have some concerning news to share with you." Jade stands humbly before the great leader of the Upperworld, and yet the smug grin threatening to spread across her face tells a different story.

"Speak, Head Sorter. What is the matter at hand?"

Jade shifts her weight from one foot to the other, trying to seem innocent even though she is about to cause more trouble than she probably should. "You are familiar with the recently-formed sorter, Delphine, correct?"

Zephyr slowly nods, his pale skin and flaming hair moving ever so slightly as his gaze meets hers with a powerful stare. "She was, well, she was a mistake."

His dark eyes become even more pitch black. "Well, I was aware of her terrible misfortune regarding Luna and that awful fiasco, but was there something else?" Jade half nods, but then pauses, placing her words carefully to keep him as calm as possible, so she can get what she wants out of this deal: justice for the rules in place.

"Well, not entirely. There is something related to this... she was - is, *unable* to sort the orbs." Zephyr's eyes grow wide. He opens his vast, cavernous mouth to speak, but then restrains himself as recognition appears in his eyes as a knowing glimmer.

"Jade, thank you for telling me this, but there is nothing I can do or say about the matter. Thank you for your time." Jade's mouth falls open.

"What? That's it? You mean, there is a sorter that was unable to sort, and you are not concerned about that? Do you care that Onyx and Evander placed her on Earth without your permission?"

Zephyr registers a look of surprise on his otherwise stone-cold, emotionless face, but then his face visibly relaxes as his long, lanky, oddly poised body relaxes soundlessly against the back of his throne. "I usually do not tolerate major decisions being made without clearance, but for this, I will make an exception. There are... circumstances that you are not permitted to know, which make this arrangement quite beneficial for all those involved."

Jade is rendered speechless, as the reaction she so desperately craved from Zephyr was not given to her, a direct blow to her ever-growing ego. But then another thought begins to take shape in her mind, the synapses connecting in her brain the way a spiderweb catches its victim suddenly, and without warning.

"Well, what would you say if I told you that they sent Delphine to Earth in order to take Luna's place?"

Zephyr's body tenses now, his dark eyes intensely searching Jade's for answers. "Nonsense! That would never be permitted."

Jade doesn't bother to fight the smug smile spreading across her lips. Now it's *her* moment. "Oh, but they did. *And...* they plan to bring Luna back to the Upperworld... even with the humanoid fetus growing inside her."

The flames seem to ignite as Zephyr takes in the revelation that Jade has provided him with. "That is impossible. I will not stand to let the Upperworld be corrupted by that unborn child."

"I couldn't agree with you more. What would you suggest that I do, my leader?" Zephyr's face takes on an even darker hue, as if he had the power to absorb every dark and troubling emotion ever felt by anyone who ever lived.

"There's nothing *you* will be doing, Jade, besides your usual job." Jade opens her mouth to protest but stops as Zephyr raises one wiry, pale finger into the tepid, foggy air. "But I will arrange for her immediate demise."

Jade tries to nod solemnly, but is then hit with the gut-wrenching realization of what this meant. She bows respectfully, but nearly falls over from her unstable state of mind. She exits the grand hall, but barely gets to the main pathway before her breathing intensifies and she is forced to sit down next to an artificially-grown tree. With her head in her hands, her mind wanders a mile a minute.

What have I done?

✳✳✳

Delphine takes her human shape underneath a tree, discreetly hidden behind a strategically-placed trashcan. She's breathing heavily, as Earth's atmosphere is so vastly different than that of the tepid, perfectly-balanced air of the Upperworld. As her heartbeat regains a normal rhythm,

167

she taps the faint green light embedded under the soft skin of her inner wrist.

"Hello? I'm here… I made it. What do I do now?" She waits a veritable eternity before she hears the familiar voice of Evander transmit to her from the only home she has ever known. "Delphine, glad you're all right. Okay, so Miranda lives in the house directly across the street. We've navigated you to her approximate location for convenience." Delphine nods, before she realizes that they cannot see her. "Okay, and then what do I do when I get there?" "You need to mention Anthony's name to her, maybe see how she reacts to the idea of him. Luna has already planted the idea on her head, now you just have to water it."

"Okay, I believe I understand. But Evander? Who is my contact? You said there would be someone I could meet with who would help me?"

"Oh my, I nearly forgot. There is a woman with brown hair sitting on the bench over by the payphone. She is one of our Undercover Earth Guardians, known as a UEG. She will provide you with shelter and food until you are established on your own. Her name is Elizabeth."

"Okay, thank you Evander." Evander sighs to himself from his posh habitation pod in the Upper World, and then steels himself for what he has to say next.

"Delphine, you should also know that your embedded communication device will be rejected from your body in about twenty Earth hours. At that point, I will no longer be able to speak to you directly. If you have any questions, you must ask them soon." Delphine chokes back some tears threatening to splash down the side of her face at the thought of losing Evander forever - he was the only real friend she'd ever known. Well, besides Luna, of course. She had made the ultimate sacrifice for Delphine - and now she was repaying the favor.

"Okay, I'll keep that in mind. Evander, if I don't get to speak to you again, thank you for everything." Now Evander is the one who must console himself in the face of losing one of his charges to the vast expanse of unforgiving Earth and its harsh environment. "It was my honor, Delphine, to serve you. I wish you all the best in your new life on Earth." And then Evander clicked off his communication device, very well knowing that he would not speak to Delphine again.

CHAPTER 10

Anthony hands Luna a piece of pizza on a paper plate as Felicia chatters happily about her day in kindergarten. "... and then, I built a giant castle out of blocks! You would have loved it, Anthony." The boy smiles at his little sister. "I bet I would have. What did Miss Suzy say about it?" Felicia grins. "She gave me a star sticker for the wall chart - and I'm the only one she gave it to today." "That's awesome, Fel!" He pats her on her head and then resumes eating his own pizza.

"Uh, aren't you hungry, Luna?" He subtly glances down at her slightly swollen belly. "You better eat something." Luna slowly nods. "I've never had this... pizza... before." Anthony tilts his head to the side. "Wow, what were you, living under a rock?" Luna's face doesn't register his joke. "Oh, I'm sorry, I just meant... who the heck has never tried pizza before? Just take a bite, it's good I promise."

"Yeah, it's my favorite!" Felicia chimes in with a big tomato-sauce smile outlining the edges of her lips. Luna smiles sweetly and then takes a bite. "Pretty good, right?" She nods, since her mouth is now full of the cheesy, melted goodness.

"All right, so do you have everything you need? The bathroom is right across the hall, and you know where your bed is. I'll be in my room right here if you need anything." Luna glances gratefully over the blankets and

170

soft pajamas that Anthony found for her on her soft bed. "Those pajamas were... my mom's. But they should fit you. You'll be more comfortable in them than that tight jumpsuit you always wear. Okay, I'll see you in the morning. Goodnight, Luna."

"Hey what about me?" Anthony is rattled from his concerns for Luna by Felicia's tight hug around his waist. "Oh no, did I forget you, Fel? My bad. I promise it won't happen again!" The little girl giggles as her brother tickles her very-vulnerable sides. "Okay, now go to bed. You have school tomorrow!" She giggles some more and then accepts defeat, walking slowly to her bed and letting Anthony tuck her in. He kisses her forehead and then exits the room, flicking off the light switch as he goes. Luna takes one look at the bedclothes Anthony had provided for her, but she opts to remain in her clothes from the Upperworld, as they make her feel much more at home in an uncertain place.

Luna closes her eyes, preparing herself to get some sleep, but sleep runs from her. She has nothing but terrible flashbacks of her recent assault, which increase her heart rate until she can barely breathe. Suddenly the tiny room she was sharing with Felicia seemed to close in on her, her mind attacking her very being. Without any better solutions presenting themselves to her, Luna decides to run outside to find solace underneath the bright stars. She gets outside and finds a good spot to look up at the sky, allowing the stars to bathe her in their bright, shining glory, making her problems seem so far away. Feeling at peace is something she always associates with lights, be it the calming hum of her bedroom light in her habitation pod, or the artificial light present in the sky of the Upperworld. Having never gotten the chance to appreciate the natural light of a starry sky and the moon, until this moment, left her breathless - their perfection could not be denied. Her breathing begins to slow as she allows herself to breathe in the crisp night air and bask in the light, until the moment when two very *unnatural* lights hit her square in the gut, knocking her flat onto the cold ground, unconscious.

✳✳✳

"Onyx, I can't imagine how you got through this... this horrendous loss. I just... I feel like I failed my job as a guide. I feel like... like I failed *her*." Onyx nods slowly, patting Evander gingerly on the back as he slowly tries to bring himself to a state of reconciliation with the fact that Delphine must now live out her life on Earth in Luna's place.

"Who says I'm through it? Evander, it's... worse for me. Now that I know, what I know. About my intended reality with her that never came to pass due to circumstances that I could not have controlled."

Evander slowly nods, but his own loss is clouding his thinking. "You know, in the 375 years of my existence, nothing of this sort has ever happened. Any idea what's going on?" Onyx looks off into the distance. "Well, I can't

172

be sure, but I've been researching some fairly interesting, albeit concerning, things from eons past." Evander makes eye contact with Onyx, awaiting more of an explanation.

"Well, what was it about?" Onyx gulps, and then turns on the temporary noise silencing device that he secretly installed on his embedded wrist device to conceal their conversation from any listening ears. "Well, for one, leaders like Zephyr are not immortal and ageless as we are." The blood visibly drains from Evander's face. "So… if that is true, what does that mean? For us? For the entire human race?" Onyx looks out the pod window wistfully, wishing with all his might that he didn't have to say the words he was about to. "Zephyr is degenerating, and will eventually perish."

Evander gasps, and begins to show signs of utter distress. "Calm down, Evander. It is not an immediate threat, but if it is true, then we have an explanation for the mix-up with Delphine." The other guide slowly calms down, and then stabilizes his breathing long enough to ask the next burning question to leap off of his tongue.

"So, what *do* you think happened with Delphine? We know about you and Luna, but what do you think is her origin? Is she even from here?" Onyx looks down at his boot-clad feet, searching for an answer that doesn't truly exist. At least not yet.

"Well, if you want my opinion… No. I do not believe that her origins are from the chemical depositories of the Upperworld's utero labs. She is much too lacking in a key ability to be a sorter - there is no way she was meant for that incredibly critical job." Evander scratches his chin.

"Well, neither you or Luna are originally from here, but you are both incredibly able to sort orbs. What is the difference, do you think?"

"That much, I haven't quite figured out yet. There is more research that I need to do first." Evander solemnly nods. "Okay, I see. Well, we've got to focus on the task at hand - getting Luna to safety, back here." Onyx nods in approval, even though the nagging thought in the back of his mind that says neither him nor Luna truly belong here, never truly stops tormenting him. However, before he can get too deep into his silent discussion, his wrist beeps green.

"Hello? Yes, thank you. I'll be right there." He squeezes his own wrist once more to end the call. "I've got to report to the utero lab for yet another recruit. I'll talk to you later, Evander. And please, for the sake of the entire human race, please remain calm. I will continue to search for answers, as long as you keep a low profile and keep doing your job."

"Yes, I believe I can manage that." Onyx nods in approval. "I'm glad to hear that."

CHAPTER 11

"So, uh Elizabeth. Are you able to tell me where I can find Miranda and Anthony?" Delphine turns her attention to her new guide as they both ride in the car on the way to Elizabeth's house for the evening.

"Yes, of course. Evander has provided me with all of that information. Although, on Earth, we are bound by a daytime and nighttime, so now we must go to my home and sleep. I've prepared the guest room for you, I think you should be comfortable there. We'll have to make other arrangements for you as well, like applying for citizenship and getting you a social security number. But that's down the road. Right now, please just try to relax. I'll help you find them both tomorrow. Oh, and we'll have to buy you some more Earth-looking clothes too..."

Delphine tries to nod politely, considering all that Elizabeth was doing for her. But there was just so much on her mind, and at the moment, tuning her out while staring out the car window into the darkness is incredibly soothing on her frazzled nerves.

"And... we're here! Come along, Delphine." Elizabeth leads her out of her small, red car and into a small, ranch-style home. A scruffy dog runs out of the house to greet them, but Delphine gets scared of even a friendly face. She has never seen a dog before.

"Oh, please don't worry! That's just Snuggles, my schnauzer. He's super friendly, I promise! Go ahead and pat him if you want." Delphine stops panicking just long enough to make eye contact with the dog. She reaches her hand to pat him, and suddenly, Snuggles growls and nips at her hand, drawing a small bead of blood. Delphine yelps, while Elizabeth yells at Snuggles.

"Snuggles! Bad dog, get in the house, now! I cannot believe he did that, I swear he has never bitten anyone before, how strange! Here, I have some bandages in the kitchen, let's get that cleaned up." Delphine began to cry from the pain, but she is also enthralled by the crimson liquid oozing out of her pure white skin. She caught herself staring at it longingly, almost sad to see Elizabeth wipe it away and cover the small wound with a bandage.

"So, you should know, that you aren't immortal like you were before. Living on Earth comes with a bunch of new threats that you likely were not aware of before." Delphine slowly nods. "How long have you..." "Lived here?" Elizabeth finishes her sentence quite accurately, as she can only imagine what Delphine is thinking all too well. "It feels like yesterday, but in reality, I suppose it's been about twenty-three Earth years. Time exists here, and moves quite quickly." Delphine nods. "Are you doing okay, sweetie? I can only imagine how hard this must be for you. Evander tells me that you weren't quite cut out for sorting?" Delphine looks down at her feet and nods. "Well that is rather unheard-of. But I believe that everything happens for a reason. You'll find your niche, I really do believe that, and you should too."

"Elizabeth? Did Evander tell you... *everything*?" Elizabeth slowly nods with a sheepish smile. "Yes, but I really don't want you to feel ashamed. That's over and done with now, so you can move on. And I must say, it was so brave of you to agree to live here, in Luna's place. My circumstances for coming here were different, as I was bred and trained for this exact purpose."

"I just... hope she can return home after all of this. I know some stuff kind of happened, but I still hope they can figure out a way to get her back. She was, is... so gifted with sorting. And I'm obviously... not." Elizabeth nods. "Well, everyone is different. Although I sure do wonder how the heck they messed up this badly..." Delphine nods, and then begins to softly cry. "Oh, darling, come here..." Elizabeth wastes no time in enveloping Delphine in a big hug. "You still have so much to look forward to, my dear. I promise you, life here will be good. Not as bad or terrifying as they may have made it seem to you, okay? We'll ease you in. Luckily, I have a lot of connections with the big-wigs who carry out the yearly census, so we'll just say you're my long-lost niece, okay? Really, I've already thought of everything, please don't worry..."

But Delphine wasn't crying about the prospects of living on Earth. Certainly, that was likely part of it, but she was primarily wondering about her identity. Why did the dog bite her? Why does it seem that no matter where she is, in the Upperworld or on Earth, it's as if she doesn't seem to fit? It's certainly not her pale pink hair, as

Elizabeth assured her that pastel hair colors are very "in" right now. That's a good thing, considering that her hair seems to grow in naturally with a pinkish hue - so she's at least a stylish freak of nature - at least that's what Delphine is telling herself.

***

Anthony awakens from a deep sleep by the screech of a car and a blood-curdling scream just outside his window. He figures out that Luna is in trouble within just a few seconds of the incident. He wastes no time in grabbing his coat and running outside to investigate, not bothering to wake up Felicia, as not to scare her until he is sure what is going on.

He rips open the front door and tears down the driveway to see a most gruesome scene: A large, bald, concerned truck driver is standing over Luna with a flashlight in one hand, and a cell phone in the other, calling 911.

"I was just driving the truck back to the depot when I swear, this little girl comes out of nowhere! I... I still don't know how I didn't see her, or what she was doing walking in the middle of the road in the middle of the night."

Anthony pushes the truck driver and his various explanations out of the way to lean down and try to revive Luna. Her face is scratched up, but it's nothing compared to the impact wounds on her torso, which are apparent even through her jumpsuit, as blood has already soaked through in three different places.

"CALL 911, YOU IDIOT! DON'T JUST STAND THERE! You're lucky I don't call the cops!" "I did, I just did... I'm, I'm so sorry. I had no idea..." Then Anthony tries to get her attention. "Luna, Luna, CAN YOU HEAR ME? LUNA!" He starts crying, his tears disappearing through the sheets of rain now falling over him. Sirens in the distance offer him some relief, that at least help is on the way. But at the moment, realizing that he might have lost Luna forever... well, it affects him more than it logically probably should have. Anthony continues to cry, whether from fear and distress, or the harsh realization that he has fallen in love with Luna, even within just a few short days. It's ridiculous, preposterous. But now he's sure. He's sure of it as he rakes his fingers through her long, raven-black hair, once voluminous, now soaked with blood and caked with wet dirt.

CHAPTER 12

Onyx approaches the utero chamber for the umpteenth time since Luna's banishment. It's killing him slowly, every time he has to help another recruit adjust to life in the Upperworld, since Luna was *supposed* to be here too. It's interesting how his focus has changed from being upset and shocked about the radical discovery of his own origin, but now, all he can think about is Luna. Per usual, Onyx manages to shove his feelings deep under the surface, hoping that they stay put until he gets back to the safety of his pod where he can properly vent. Trying to live in this mechanistic environment, with excess human emotion still in him, is more of an impediment than it may appear.

He raises his forearm over the sensor of the chamber, until it blinks green and opens, granting him access to the rapidly-growing recruit in the beginning stages of the light-gathering process. He walks in and sits on the floor next to the tall, clear cylinder holding the beginnings of a new sorter. The pale, almost pink blob of flesh floating in the nutrition-packed fluid vibrates slightly, and Onyx watches it grow with zero interest in the process. He's been watching this happen for over four hundred Earth years, after all. Right now, he just sits, and waits, for the cylinder to eventually drain and deposit the fetus on the floor next to him as a fully-formed being, within about an hour.

In the time it takes for the being to fully form, Onyx breathes deeply and tries to center himself, as he must remain calm in order to comfort the new recruit. The amount of emotional energy it takes for him to both hide his traumatized state, as well as provide stability and guidance for another individual, is incredibly taxing. He can feel his body heaving, his heart beating loudly in his ears, but he fights to gain control of his own heightened emotions.

Forty-nine minutes and thirty-two seconds to go. Onyx leans his head against the smooth, white, sterile wall of the utero chamber and tries to relax. As if in response to his internal pain, the fetus in the cylinder gurgles, a typical side-effect of excess air in the forming process. But somehow, Onyx feels threatened by this simple, natural process. The hairs on the back of his neck stand up straight, as if something quite evil was gaining life through that tube. Onyx quickly tries to shake off the feeling though. It is infinitely more probably that his lack of sleep mixed with internal emotional pain was just beginning to take its toll on him. At least, that's what he tells himself.

✳✳✳

Overtaken by his own curiosity about Delphine's odd inability to sort, Evander decides to ask Jade if she knows anything about it. It is likely a futile attempt at gaining insight, as Jade knew about both Onyx's and Luna's rather unorthodox entry into the Upperworld, yet she was sworn to secrecy about it as Primary Guide. Well, he himself was the appointed Treasurer of the Upperworld, so maybe, just maybe, he had enough clout to get something out of her, if only he could figure out the best way to ask.

Once he gets up enough confidence, Evander makes his way to Jade's habitation pod. Before he can change his mind, he swiftly pushes the small button next to her automated door, notifying her of his presence. A small green light responds to his presence, signaling him to let himself in. Evander hesitantly does so, and after walking through Jade's incredible sterile, organized living area, he finds her in the kitchen area reading the latest issue of the Upperworld's newspaper. Her immaculately-painted fingernails glow eerily in the low light, a very pale blue.

"Oh, hello Evander. I was just, sitting here. Doing nothing. Catching up on reading, you know, the usual. Since I'm off work, at the moment." Evander is immediately taken aback by her uncharacteristic rambling. Not much can cause Jade to become unglued.

"Um, Jade, is everything okay?" Jade nods her head rapidly, with much enthusiasm, as if to be compensating for something subconsciously.

"Oh yes, right as rain, or so I've heard. Isn't that what the humanoids are saying these days?" Evander is now even more taken aback by her eerily sunny disposition, but tries to brush it aside as he is here on a much more important mission.

"Well, as the Treasurer, I've recently realized that there is a small breach in my records..." Jade nods.

"Oh, is that so?"

"Yes, and I was wondering if, you would be able to provide me with the missing information?"

Jade nods emphatically. "Absolutely. What are you looking for?" She immediately walks over to her main computer stashed discretely in one of the kitchenette cabinets.

Evander gulps, willing both air and saliva to satiate the growing lump in the back of his throat. "Well, I have no records on the origin of Delphine." He notices Jade's shoulders briefly stiffen, ever so slightly, and just for a split second, but they quickly relax, and she turns around with a plastic smile stuck on her face.

"Sure... just give me a moment to pull up the official document. I am surprised you didn't have it before, but I'll print it out for you so you can file it away in the archives, if you like." Evander nods, surprised at how easy this was.

"Yes, that would be quite useful. Thank you, Jade." She doesn't respond, but instead just turns around, hands him the paper, and not-so-subtly guides him out her front door. When he is about to turn around to leave, Jade breaks her sparkling facade just for a moment, long enough to say: "Read this in the privacy of your pod, and *do not* share this information with anyone." His face freezes, as hers regains its composure. "Talk to you later, Evander. Have a great day!" Then she waves, and shuts her door with a thud. And the weirdest thing about the entire interaction may have been that last portion. *Jade never waves… to anyone. What's her deal? I bet she's hiding something. Something big.*

CHAPTER 13

After what feels like a small eternity, the flashing lights and sounds in the distance finally make their way to where Anthony is crouched over Luna, while the truck driver who hit her stands there in a silent panic.

As the ambulance pulls right over to them, Anthony barely gets to say a word before Luna's small, frail, body is lifted by the larger, burly EMTs. Her damp hair cascades away from her neck, until it finally lands on the sterile, white pillow stationed on the gurney. They're about to close the doors, until Anthony realizes that he has no idea which hospital they are going to.

"Hey, where are you taking her? Can I ride with you?" One of the EMTs looks over in his direction, while yelling through the rain. "Are you family?" Anthony scratches the back of his head. "Well, no, not by blood. But -"

"No 'buts'. If you're not related, you can't ride in the ambulance with her. You'll have to meet us at the hospital in the next town over." Anthony breathes a sigh of relief, as he knew where that was. "Okay, thank you." He begins to run to his car, but realizes that he needs his keys, and to bring Felicia with him. In a frenzied panic, he runs back inside the house and tries to calmly wake up Felicia, preferably without showing how scared he truly is.

"Hey, Fel... I need you to come with me to the hospital..."

"Uhhh, what? I was sleeping, Anthony."

"I know, but Luna's been hurt and I have to get to the hospital, so I'm taking you with me. Hurry up and grab your coat and shoes."

"But my pajamas…"

"Pajamas are fine, Fel. Just bundle up, it's chilly out there."

Within a few minutes, Anthony and Felicia get into the car and make their way to the hospital. The rain and wind outside whips against the windshield as the two ride in a stunned silence.

"Anthony?" He looks back at Felicia by looking up at the rearview mirror.

"Yeah Fel?"

"Do you think Luna is going to be okay?"

Anthony takes a long, deep breath in and slowly exhales out through rounded lips.

"Honestly, I don't know, Fel. She is hurt really, really bad. But I sure do hope she'll be okay."

Felicia nods, her long curly hair illuminated by the passing streetlights as they make their way to the hospital.

Once at the hospital, Anthony grasps Felicia's sweaty palm in his own, and saunters over to the front desk as calmly as possible.

"Welcome to Oak Memorial Hospital. How can I help you?" The woman at the front desk wears black-rimmed glasses that sit securely at the base of a pointed nose, which make her appear rather bird-like.

"Hi, I'm looking for a girl recently brought by ambulance to the emergency room, she goes by the name of Luna, but she was unconscious after being hit by a truck."

The receptionist doesn't so much as bat an eyelash at his sensitive query, but rather checks her database on the computer without saying a word.

"Ah yes, it seems that she is now in the urgent care facility. You'll need to take a left down that hallway, and then take the elevator to floor 3."

"Thank you. Come on, Felicia."

✳✳✳

Onyx tries to steady his frayed nerves by breathing deeply as the utero chamber begins to open, revealing the unconscious body of his next recruit. In a matter of minutes, the recruit would awaken, and Onyx would be the one to guide him through all the things he would need to know as a sorter. The exhaust from the chamber cast an eerie fog over the room, and Onyx still can't shake the feeling that something is very, very wrong.

He steels himself to begin instruction by getting a look at his newest recruit. His hair is dark black, and his skin is very pale, and delicate. Onyx stares at the blank, sterile, white wall, waiting for the recruit to awaken. His mind takes him to his most major worry - Luna. He hasn't heard anything about her, since the natural insemination, but that was all he had to know - she wouldn't be allowed back to the Upperworld because of it. But luckily, Evander said he was working on a way to get her back, regardless of her physical state. Nothing was proven or guaranteed though, and Onyx makes the constant mistake of letting himself imagine the worst. His worries and pain are what keep him up at night, and there is never a sure way to alleviate that anxiety.

"Uh, h…hello?" Onyx turns his head as his new recruit sits up, repeatedly blinking his eyes to adjust to the harsh fluorescent lighting of the utero chamber.

"Hello, my name is Onyx and I'll be your guide…" He begins his litany of instructions, still staring at the wall. Onyx knows all too well that getting emotionally attached to a recruit is never a good idea.

"But, why does the light hurt so bad?" Onyx turns to look him in the eye to answer his question, but that is the first mistake he makes.

The recruit's eyes are a bright shade of… violet.

VOLUME THREE:
THE CHILD

CHAPTER 1

He freezes mid-thought, not even bothering to keep to the same script he always used with new recruits.

"What? How? Who are you?"

He tilts his head slightly. "Um, I have no idea. I just... I just woke up? Is that what you'd call it? I feel like I... I fell asleep."

"You can already speak? And you don't feel any pain from the light-gathering process?"

He shakes his head. "None at all. I just remember being somewhere warm and snug, and then nothingness, and now I'm here."

Onyx's face goes pale. "Let me scan your forearm." Onyx removes the scanner from his utility belt, to find out the name of this new recruit.

The scanner buzzes loudly, and a red warning signal fills the screen:

WARNING: SYSTEM FAILURE
RETRACTED HUMANOID PROGENY OF ANOTHER
RETRACTED HUMANOID HAS ENTERED THE
UPPERWORLD
MONIKER: SETH
NO HUMANOID # AVAILABLE
MATERNAL
HUMANOID#4683929749857397562888
393028

Onyx falls to his knees as a wave of realization washes over him… his gut had been right. Something was very, very wrong. Then he runs as fast as he can out of the utero chamber, to nowhere in particular. He just has to get away.

Luna's unborn child had died, and ended up in the Upperworld? But how? And why?

✳✳✳

Evander re-enters his own habitation pod with the missing information about Delphine's history in his hand. He unfurls it without any hesitation, except for some curiosity about why Jade handed it to him so willingly, and then seemed utterly concerned that he keep it a secret. It only takes a moment for him to quickly understand why.

NON-HUMANOID ORIGIN
ALTERNATE PLACE OF ORIGIN: TARTARUS
REASON FOR UPPERWORLD PLACEMENT:
SYSTEM ERROR
SHADOW #66666666666
MONIKER: DELPHINE

His hands quickly begin to shake, realizing what this could mean for not only the Upperworld, but also human history.

That's why she couldn't see the glow of an orb… she is a DEMON.

Evander shakes his head, blinking at the revelation he held in his hands about that poor, not-so-innocent girl that he had so desperately tried to help. It is becoming all too much, much too fast. Little does he know that Onyx had also discovered something terrible about his previous charge. Between both situations, Onyx and Evander are about to have to fight forces much bigger than just some unruly humans. Very possibly, they'd be dealing with something as difficult and complicated as the forces of good and evil.

And on top of it all, Miranda and Anthony are still living lives away from each other.

✳✳✳

"But why must she be destroyed? She hasn't done anything except what she's been told..." Jade stands resolutely in front of Zephyr, shamelessly pleading with him to let Luna carry on without a threat. "It wasn't her fault, what happened, you know..."

Zephyr's cold stare remains resolutely focused on Jade's opposing snarl.

"Be that as it may, she has been irrevocably damaged, and is thus no use to us here. There is simply nothing I can do, you see, plans have already been put into place, Jade."

At that moment, Jade's head snaps out of her smug tilt and to complete attention, awaiting Zephyr's explanation for such a radical claim.

"What kinds of plans?"

Zephyr cracks his pale, wiry knuckles in the dim light of the Grand Hall. "Well, you may not be aware, but I've arranged for her undead fetus to be absorbed into the utero lab, with some consciousness intact. He has been re-formed, and I will have him brought here for a de-briefing momentarily. As soon as that is accomplished, he will be sent back to Earth to carry out my plan for me."

"I'm not sure I understand."

Zephyr allowed an all-knowing smile to ooze across his putrified lips. "*You* don't have to know anything. I'll take care of all the details, no need to worry. She'll be dead within two Earth days."

Jade's blood runs cold as her face turns pale. She wants to react, but knows that would only make things worse for her, and for the others.

"Okay, *my leader*, I'll get back to work then." Zephyr nods approved dismissal. As Jade slowly walks down the cold, darkened hallway, she realizes the obvious.

I need to tell Onyx that Luna is in grave danger... and that maybe he's the only one who can save her.

The enormity of the problem was really beginning to shake Jade's focus, which is a problem as she holds a coveted leadership position in the Upperworld. She refuses to back down whenever things get tough. But in her own defense, things had never been this tough before.

CHAPTER 2

Delphine sleeps fitfully, even in the nice room that Elizabeth had provided for her. Snuggles had been locked in his crate after the biting and growling incident, but Delphine still does not feel safe. There was no logical reason why not, and it was more likely that she is just frightened after being sent away from the one home she ever knew.

But there was something else too. It seems that being on Earth has this different effect on her, as if she has this insatiable desire... no, a need... to connect with the ground. Or better yet, below the ground. Something about going deeper seemed to feel like home to her. Not that she's ever been below ground, but she could sense a sort of presence, or rather, a humming, deep below the surface. She doesn't know what to do with this thought, or what it means (if anything at all).

After an unknown amount of time, Delphine finally falls asleep, but then wakes up to the sound of a barking dog. Elizabeth opens her bedroom door at that moment, as if to apologize for the noise.

"I'm sorry he's so loud. It's just... he's not used to being crated, and he's hungry for breakfast. Go ahead and get ready to leave - I'm going to take you to Miranda's approximate location so you can assess how to get her to Anthony. I'm not sure how, but I'm just doing what Evander told me to have you do ASAP. Then after that, we can go shopping for some more Earthly clothes for you. How does that sound?"

Delphine nods calmly at her attempt at welcoming her. Elizabeth was so kind to take her in and help her the way she was, but with every passing moment, Delphine was beginning to realize that she was grasping her mission less and less. She knows consciously that Anthony and Miranda were separated accidentally and must be reunited, but somehow, that seems so far away, when all she really wants to do is explore the depths of the dark, soil-covered Earth.

Temporarily avoiding such vagrant thoughts, Delphine forces herself to remain focused on the task at hand as she gets into Elizabeth's car and they drive to some unknown location.

"So Miranda's house is just a street away from here. I'll be able to take you over there because I've set the pretense that you're new in town and I wanted you to meet some of the locals. Trust me, that'll make sense. Almost everyone knows everyone around here - except for people who live out of town, like Anthony."

But Delphine is barely listening at all - she is too distracted by the humming of the baked asphalt underneath the car's tires.

"And... we're here! So here's what I think might work. Here is a notecard with Anthony's contact info. I need you to say he's a friend of yours who works at the minimart near the park..."

"But I've never met Anthony!"

"Doesn't matter. Trust me on this. It's going to take a while to get them together, but you've got to start somewhere. Evander tells me that they have at least met a couple times, thanks to Luna, so that'll make things easier for us."

Delphine slowly nods, even though this "plan" is sounding crazier and crazier every second.

"Okay, I'll try it. You'll come with me, right?"

Elizabeth nods.

"Okay then."

Elizabeth rings the doorbell of Miranda's house, and after a moment, the door opens to reveal a very casually-dressed Miranda in loose sweatpants and a tank top. Her hair is up in a loose bun, and there's a scowl on her face."

"What."

"Oh, I'm sorry, is this a bad time? My name is Elizabeth Willard, and this is my niece, Delphine. She'll be living with me and she's new in town, so I was bringing her around to meet some neighbors." With a not-so-subtle nudge, Elizabeth guides Delphine in front of her so she is face-to-face with Miranda herself.

"Well, welcome, I guess."

"Thank you! Here is the contact info of Anthony… you might like him." Delphine shoves the index card desperately into Miranda's outstretched hand.

"Ugh, well, Delphine is just very… sociable. She's always trying to play matchmaker, silly girl."

196

Despite Elizabeth's attempt to ameliorate the situation, Miranda still wears a scowl on her face.

"Um, I'm just getting off of a really tough... thing... that happened... so I'm really not into meeting anyone right now. But thanks, I guess."

She closes the front door with a thud, as the index card flutters to the ground mercilessly at Delphine's boot-clad feet.

"Did I say something wrong?" Elizabeth pats her on the shoulder as they walk back to the car. "It just takes time to adjust to the social climate here. You'll find your way soon enough. I had to - I was once just as uncomfortable here as you, believe it or not."

"So now what?"

"Now we go shopping!"

CHAPTER 3

"Hi, I'm looking for a girl…"

"Aren't we all, buddy."

"No, she's… hurt. She was hit by a truck. Long, dark hair…"

"Not very specific, I'm going to need a name."

"Uh, Luna."

"Luna… what?" At that moment, Anthony realizes that she never told him her last name.

"Uh, I don't actually know. I'll just, take a walk around and look for her myself. Come on, Fel."

After a very panicked walk around the third floor intensive care unit, Anthony is about to abandon all hope when he finally sees Luna's characteristic long, dark, hair flowing daintily over a pillow case.

She's still unconscious, but there are tubes and various monitors attached all over her body. The nurses likely stripped her tight restrictive jumpsuit off of her, as she now wears a typical hospital gown. Although Anthony noticed the bright pink glow of her neon jumpsuit even through the white drawstring bag labeled "patient belongings" plopped on the side table next to her bed.

A nurse enters the curtained-off area of the unit with a clipboard and a stethoscope around her neck. Upon eye contact with Anthony, her lips form a soft "o" and she forces a small, comforting smile.

"Oh my, are you the father?"

"Me? What? No. It's not mine. Of course not, I'm just... a friend that she's staying with right now."

She nods solemnly. "Well, that's a relief, as the prognosis isn't good."

"What? No, don't tell me she's... not going to make it..."

The nurse opens her mouth to say something, and then stops. "Oh, the girl? She's expected to make a full recovery. She's only sleeping - regained consciousness maybe half an hour ago. I meant... the baby... is gone. Miscarriage upon impact, looks like."

Anthony's eyes widen, as if in preparation for a wall of emotions to hit, but he feels nothing. He just calmly nods and leads Felicia to a nearby seat.

"Here, Fel. You're probably tired so try and relax in this chair, okay? I brought your favorite stuffed animals in this backpack."

Felicia nods sleepily and settles herself in the chair, resting her head on the wall behind her, cuddling a stuffed bear.

Anthony buries his head in his hands, feeling upset at himself for the amount of relief he feels at the news of the baby being gone. For Luna's sake, she was attacked, and now she wouldn't have to live a life with a reminder of that. It's terribly unfortunate that the accident with the truck occurred, but he's comforted with the news that she seems to be on her way to a full recovery.

✳✳✳

In his moment of panic, Onyx decides to run to Jade. He rings her doorbell, but she isn't there. *I better check the Sorting Room, she's probably working.* He wastes no time running there next, quickly spying the back of Jade's characteristically dyed silver hair tied into a neat bun.

"Oh, hello Onyx. Something I can do-"

"Luna's fetus was destroyed and somehow ended up here, in the utero chamber. It didn't even go through the system, when I scanned his arm, an error message came up. This isn't... protocol. I have no idea what to do."

Jade's eyes widened, as she begins to realize that Zephyr's plan was beginning to come to fruition. They had to act, and they had to act *fast*.

"Onyx, we need to talk." She turns to her assistant and barks some instructions to be carried out in her absence, and then guides Onyx out of the Sorting Room.

"What? Do you know something that I don't?"

Jade slowly nods. "I had spoken to Zephyr, because I was concerned about Luna. I... I didn't want any harm, I promise..."

"Jade, *what did you do...*"

Her normally calm gray eyes begin to grow red and watery.

"I... I somehow made him think that she should be destroyed."

"You did *WHAT?*"

200

Jade nods, the words were failing to move past the tip of her tongue and instead began choking her from the inside out.

"I can't even remember what I said, but he's... going to have her destroyed."

"How? When?"

"Zephyr said something about her fetus being used against her, I think? I can barely remember."

Onyx drops to his knees and begins to choke on his own words. "Jade, I need to know where, how, and what. And then... then I need to get to Earth. I'll protect her myself."

"What? But Zephyr said-"

Onyx mumbled a few words characteristic of Earthly profanity that he likely picked up during his century of humanoid studies. "I don't care. Get me to Earth, and I honestly don't even care if I ever come back, at this point. I really need your help here, Jade."

Everything Jade had been trained to do, causes her to want to question everything he was asking her to do. None of this is protocol, but then again, neither is destroying a sorter through her own undead fetus. With that logic, Jade nods her head slowly, and agrees to get Onyx to Earth.

"But, what's your plan?"

Onyx looks off into the hazy purple sky of the Upperworld. "Well, I'll find Luna, and protect her from Seth."

"Who?"

"Her fetus. You said Zephyr was going to use him to destroy her?"

Jade nods.

"Well, I'll keep him away from her, and protect her for the remainder of our lives on Earth."

"What? You mean you're not going to try to bring her back?"

Onyx shakes his head.

"I don't think either of us can live here, knowing what I know now, both about how badly things are run here, and the injustice. It's horrifying." he clenches his hands in anticipation.

"Well, it's certainly better than Earth...

"Is it, though? On Earth, humans live with freedom to be whatever they want to be. They can love, and give love to others. And often, as we know too well, they procreate. Don't you ever wonder what it would be like to get to control your own destiny?"

Jade shakes her head. "Uh, no. Not at all. I think that they *need* us to plan their lives for them. What would they do without us?"

"Whatever they want."

"Onyx, I don't think I've ever told you this..." Jade fights back the lump forming in her throat. "I've always admired you."

Onyx grasps her hand in solidarity. "And I, you."

"Now let's get you to Earth. I believe the transporter room is open."

"But Evander... I didn't get to say goodbye."

202

"There's no time for that! You said you saw the fetus, right? It's only a matter of time before Zephyr sends him after you both."

Onyx gazes longingly at the home he's known for his entire existence, and then deeply inhales the tepid air, as if for the very last time.

"You are right, I better go. But what will you say about my disappearance? I'll need a replacement."

"I'll take care of that, just go take care of your girl."

Onyx's face glows with the anticipation of seeing Luna again. In all the hustle of trying to protect her, he had nearly forgotten that he was meant to build a life with her all along, before the Sorting Room got in the way. In a twisted way, it is beginning to seem like the original plan for them was winning out.

"And where will you send me?"

"Since her tracking device was expelled, we haven't been able to follow her exact location. But I can send you to the spot where she was last tracked. I doubt that she could have gotten too far from there."

"Well okay then."

"And do you have Earth currency on you?

"I always do."

Though not often mentioned, it was Upperworld policy for guides to have various Earth currency on them at all times, should there arise an emergency where they would need to visit Earth. It was rare, but happened occasionally.

Jade instructs him to lie down on the table, as she made sure that he is lined up perfectly with the molecular scrambler to be reassembled on Earth.

"Okay, you'll feel a gentle itch, and then nothing at all, until you wake up on Earth. I want you to know that I believe in you, Onyx. And you will be missed."

Onyx nods, and then inhales the Upperworld's air for the truly last time, as his body feels weightless, and then nonexistent.

CHAPTER 4

Feeling especially frustrated with her recent breakup from Garth, Miranda gets herself out of bed, but only to get to the convenience store to buy more frosting and cookie batter. No matter how unhealthy it is, the gooey, sugary treat was the only thing that made her heart hurt less. She and Garth had been together for a couple years and things were perfect then, before he started doing the drugs and the alcohol. They were high school sweethearts, and they started Toxic Exposure as an act for their school talent show, before it started to get any real traction. Now they had a following, with even some people crazy enough to be groupies. But it was all down the tubes with the recent, horrific things he had done. The hitting, and the mental abuse was rightfully taking its toll on Miranda, and after she had heard what *that scoundrel* did to that poor younger girl, it was all too much to handle. She dumped his sorry ass and then blocked his number on her phone before he could harass her any further. Now, cookie batter and frosting was her muse, although not a ton of good songs could come of that, and Miranda was beginning to think her music should die *with* their relationship.

Looks like I have to go to the convenience store for more sugary stuff. Within a minute, while still in her pajamas and hoodie, Miranda grabs her purse and house keys, and begins the trek to the store down the street near the park. *Maybe a little time at the park would help me a bit,* she muses to herself. But in her heart, she knows that being seen in public without Garth by her side was mortifying. All the local fans had began to view them as a unit. Miranda was beginning to resent that, and yet she also hated the thought of being seen in her pajamas. More likely than not, she'll just get to the store, grab what she wanted, and get home.

The walk to the store is awkward for sure, as the hot sun seems to target the blackness of her worn hoodie, threatening to burn her to oblivion. She ignores it, as well as the typical catcalls, as best she can, and enters the convenience store, half expecting to see the typical cashier, Anthony, there. When he's nowhere to be found, she gets suspicious that something might be wrong, as he'd been there for the last few cookie batter and frosting runs she had to make this week. And although they weren't exactly friends, she's always seen him around town and always appreciated how courteous he was, even just in the retail atmosphere.

"Uh, excuse me, is Anthony here?" She gets the attention of the bottle-blonde manager scanning bags of potato chips. "Nope. Oh, you didn't hear? He's at the hospital, there was an accident…"

Miranda nearly inhales her own saliva. "What? Is he okay?" The blonde shrugs her shoulders. "Oh, I don't know, all he said to me was that there had been an accident. His job has been put on hold until he returns."

Miranda nods solemnly, until a thought occurs to her. "Um, do you know what hospital, he's at, exactly?"

The blonde plants a manicured talon on her popped-out hip. "Who's asking?"

Miranda pauses for a moment, frosting in hand, and says something surprising. "A friend."

The manager nods, as if to grant her access to something very exclusive and personal, and then she snaps her gum, as if to break the spell that Miranda seemingly cast over her with her little white lie. "Oak Memorial, on the other side of town."

"Great, thanks." Miranda turns to leave.

"Hey! You gotta pay for those…"

Miranda's face turns red, and she turns back to the checkout counter. "Of course, sorry about that." Then she pays for her junk food and walks to the bus stop to make her way over to the hospital.

✳✳✳

"Delphine, try on this one." The very well-meaning Elizabeth hands Delphine another sundress, but nothing she tries on feels right to her, except for the black sweaters and combat boots.

"Elizabeth, I really don't like it, it's… itching me."

Elizabeth steps behind the curtain where Delphine is trying on one dress of many, trying to assimilate into Earth culture the best she can. "Well that's weird. This one is 100% cotton, how could it be itching you? Oh well, I'll keep looking, sit tight." Elizabeth disappears yet again to go find more things for Delphine to try on, but it seems like such a losing battle.

It was hard enough walking through the mall without such strange reactions. Delphine doesn't appear all that different than anyone else, aside from the jumpsuit and pastel pink hair. But the strangest thing, is the way that any toddler or baby that she walked near would immediately start crying and run away from her. She isn't mean, and she sure doesn't look scary, but they ran from her like she was a monster, or something of that sort. Delphine manages to brush it off, thinking that perhaps it was just because she wasn't assimilated yet, and that maybe things would improve with time. Or at least, she sure hoped it would.

"Delphine, honey, try on these please!" She grabs the white pants dangling from Elizabeth's outstretched arm over the dressing room curtain. But oddly enough, she didn't have to try them on to know that they would burn her skin. Anything she tried on that wasn't black or her own jumpsuit from the Upperworld was irritating.

"Um, Elizabeth? Would you mind terribly if we just go home now? I'm really quite... tired."

"Sure, Delphine. I can imagine you would be."

Delphine grabs the rest of the discarded clothing, all while ignoring the way they made even her fingertips severely itch.

"So, perhaps just the black pants, sweaters, and boots for now?"

Delphine nods. "Sorry about everything else."

208

"Not to worry. We'll just come back another time, I can only imagine what you must be going through." Elizabeth pays for their items and then they walk back through the mall and out to her car, leaving a trail of crying toddlers and babies in their wake.

CHAPTER 5

"Anthony?" Luna wakes from her slumber, and gets his attention from her hospital bed across the little room.

"Yes? Luna? How are you, how are you feeling?"

She smiles briefly and then almost frowns, while her hand rests gently on her slightly swollen abdomen.

"They say it's... gone."

Anthony nods. "I know."

"Is that bad?"

Anthony is at a loss for words. Of course losing a baby would be considered a tragedy, but in her situation, he couldn't help but consider it to be a gracious reprieve from a life of suffering. "I don't know, Luna."

Oddly satisfied with even an indecisive answer, Luna allows herself to succumb to the sleep tugging at the corners of her eyes. She's likely tired from the trauma of everything that has happened to her. Anthony doesn't quite know everything about her, but he can sense that there are deeper secrets more wild than anything he has ever experienced in his life, hidden behind those deep violet eyes.

Anthony is pulled away from his thoughts by Felicia tugging gently on his sleeve.

"Anthony? Is she okay?"

Anthony nods. "Yes, I think so. She's just sleeping now."

Felicia nods. "Can we go home, now?"

"I have to talk to the doctor first, and then we can all go home. Wait here please."

Anthony leaves Felicia in the hospital room with Luna in the search for a nurse or doctor that has been treating Luna. He finds one nearby before too long.

"Excuse me, are you the nurse for Room 206?" The woman clad in light blue scrubs nods busily while jotting something down into a notebook.

"Yep. What do you need?"

"I was just wondering when she can be discharged. She seems okay now, just sleepy."

"We're going to need to keep her until the morning for observation. She's also got some broken bones to attend to, so the doctor said it could be a few days."

Anthony tries and fails to hide his frustration. "Okay, thank you." The nurse nods curtly before turning away to care for another patient.

I better call Tiffany to let her know that I may need a day or two off of work.

He takes out his cell phone and punches in the main phone number of his boss.

"Hi Tiffany... yes, I'm okay. She is too, just a few broken bones... But I think I may need a day or two off of work, just to take care of her and my sister... Okay, thanks... yes, I'll keep you posted... bye now."

He places his phone back into his pocket, hoping that everything will pan out quickly so that he can resume his life as usual. Well, as usual as it can be for a 19-year-old raising his little sister on his own and taking in a strange girl with a penchant for pale pink jumpsuits.

✳✳✳

Onyx finds himself on a wooden park bench, underneath a bright blue sky. *It's exactly as I've studied it... fascinating.* Rather than being scared or frightened the way most sorters might be upon a sudden and unexpected journey to Earth, he is invigorated. Unsurprisingly, he feels like he belonged there the whole time, which makes sense, since he did.

Okay, now to find Luna. I suppose I'll just have to walk around and see what I can find. He rakes his fingers through his short, bleach-blonde hair and tries to adjust to the different gravity levels as quickly as possible.

He soon recognizes the convenience store across the street, from the footage following Luna before her embedded communication device was expelled from her body. He walks casually across the street, carefully navigating through the traffic lights and pedestrians with ease. The door opens for him automatically upon his approach, and he finds a woman at the front counter who appears to be counting currency. He makes eye contact with her as he walks over.

"Hi, how can I help you?"

"I'm looking for a girl-"

"Yeah, aren't you all."

"No, I mean, a specific one. She knows one of your employees... Anthony, I think it is?"

Recognition floods her face. "Oh, I think I know who you're talking about - he recently took some girl in, saying she was hurt, lost, and needed a place to stay. He's at Oak Memorial Hospital with her now."

Hospital... I remember that term. That's for the injured. Wait a minute... Luna is injured? Did Seth already get to her?

"Oh, okay, thank you. I better get going, then." The girl nods, and then resumes her busywork at the front counter.

Okay, Earth studies, don't fail me now. Onyx considers himself extremely lucky to have had the extensive training that he did - it would make his assimilation to Earth a lot faster and easier than it would have been, had he had zero training, like Luna. *Poor Luna! It's a miracle that she survived as long as she did. But I am grateful, nonetheless. Now to get onto a... bus, I think it's called.*

Onyx finds the nearest bus stop, and pays his fare with the emergency Earth currency he carries with him always. He is unprepared for the many blank, curious stares he gets from onlookers, his pale blue jumpsuit clearly bringing a lot of unwanted attention his way.

Note to self - obtain humanoid clothes as soon as possible. Luckily, the bus ride itself was quite pleasant, even though his mind is whirring with the many possible ways that this could play out. Luna could have forgotten all about him by now, if she was even still alive.

CHAPTER 6

Jade tries to carefully walk out of the transport room with as little suspicion as possible. If Zephyr finds out about what she did, she has a gut feeling that she would be punished with something worse than death. She is about to get back to her post in the Sorting Room, but she realizes that she should talk to Evander about what has happened, as well as address the realization of who Delphine really is. And worst of all, the sheer reality that Delphine was made a sorter at all, points to some severe problems with the Upperworld itself, meaning that Zephyr himself may be deteriorating.

She tries and fails to focus on her objective at hand, which is her typical overseeing of the Sorting Room operations. Quickly realizing that she is unable to focus, which could put humanity at risk for another failed humanoid, Jade decides that it may be best to just have her assistant cover for her.

After that is settled, she walks to Evander's pod, hoping that he is doing okay with the shocking news about Delphine. It was high-clearance information, but she feels strongly that given the crazy circumstances, he has a right to know. There is just too much going on that seems beyond protocol anyway, what's one more thing?

The door opens on its own, and she walks in to find Evander sitting with his back to the wall and his head in his hands. Clearly, the news did not go down easily for him.

"Evander, are you all right? I'm just... I need to talk to you."

He barely turns his head to look at her, but the red rims around his eyes show either debilitating fear or anger. "Why did you never tell me this? That I was harboring a *demon*? Don't you think that would have been helpful for her guide to know? Heck, I shouldn't have been her guide at all - she should have stayed in Hell where she belongs!"

Jade exhales softly, searching for the right words to defuse the explosive unwittingly wired by her own design.

"I'm sorry, my loyalty is to Zephyr, I was just following orders..."

"I know, but don't you see it? Onyx sees it, I see it... the system is *breaking*. I was thinking, hoping -fa that maybe the rules wouldn't apply the same way anymore. There's just too much that's going wrong. I think we have to just do whatever it takes to save it."

"I agree with you completely. Actually, about that, you should know: Onyx is gone."

Evander is pulled out of his sobbing with this sudden news. "What do you mean, *gone*?"

"Well, he went to Earth... to protect Luna."

"Protect her from what?"

"Seth - uh, her undead fetus."

"Do you realize how ridiculous you sound right now?"

"Unfortunately, I do. But it's all very true."

"Well, when's he coming back?"

Jade fingers her silver strands of hair and avoids eye contact with him.

"He's not, is he?"

She shakes her head. "It's up to us, now, to fix things."

"You mean, to get Miranda and Anthony together?"

"Well, not entirely, Delphine will do that. I was thinking more, on a larger scale."

"Do you have a plan?"

"Not yet - I've got nothing."

✳✳✳

Delphine arrives back at Elizabeth's house, where Snuggles begins barking at her unceasingly again. He always does - it was becoming less of an oddity, and more of a routine. And that was strange. Elizabeth notices her discomfort and tries to ameliorate the situation.

"Hmmm, perhaps I can have my friend watch Snuggles for a bit, just until we get you settled in more?" She yells over the barking, an unfortunate example of the way dogs tend to sometimes control their owners. The piercing, brown eyes of the dog never leave Delphine's gaze until he is ushered back into his crate and brought out to the car.

"I'll be right back, Delphine. Please try and make yourself comfortable, I'll just bring Snuggles to Sabrina's house and then I'll be right back, okay?" Delphine nods.

"Okay, thank you."

"Anytime, Sweetie."

As Elizabeth makes her way out the front door with the dog who stops barking as soon as the door closes, Delphine plops down onto the couch in front of the television. The remote sits next to her on the side table, and after messing with the buttons for a few minutes, she turns it on, and is immediately mesmerized by the color images of people that appear.

It's just like the screens in the Upperworld.

✳✳✳

Walking down the long, cold, hallway toward Zephyr's throne, the slow, deliberate steps of Luna's scorned child approach. The cold, ashen colors of the stone corridor mix with the tepid air that grows steadily colder where Zephyr is seated.

His large, violet eyes lock into a powerful stare, challenging even Zephyr's power. But the esteemed leader of the Upperworld does not, would not, back down. This is the beginning of a collaboration, not a fight.

"Seth, I presume?"

The young recruit nods. "You summoned me here, my leader?"

"Indeed. I have something I need you to… take care of, for me." The pair of striking violet eyes, framed by hair as dark as raven's feather, widen in anticipation.

"Seth, I need you to go to Earth via the transport room, located adjacent to the Sorting Room. You'll be going to assassinate a girl who *used to* work in the Sorting Room, under the moniker 'Luna'."

"But isn't she immortal if she worked here?"

"On Earth, she is rendered mortal." Seth slowly nods, but there are still many questions floating around directly behind his violet irises.

"What method of assassination would you prefer?" Zephyr strokes his ghastly, pale, nearly translucent chin with two long, bony fingers.

"Any is fine, really. But..." He pauses for a moment, and then snaps his fingers in the foggy air. Immediately, a short, silver blade appears in his outstretched hand.

"Take this dagger, and plunge it directly into her heart. When you have accomplished that, squeeze this piece of magnetized rock three times." Zephyr hands him a small black pendant on a metal chain.

"There is a heat and pressure sensor embedded into it. Do that immediately after her demise, and then you will be able to reappear back here."

"And what would I gain from this?"

Zephyr strokes his chin in thought, and then pauses.

"Only the greatest reward of all - the opportunity to work alongside me as my primary advisor for all of eternity - a position of great power. You want that, don't you?"

Seth's eyes widen even further, and he nods excitedly.

"Thought so."

CHAPTER 7

Onyx carefully follows the map on the bus, and navigates his way to the hospital. Once inside, he nearly freezes in confusion. It is going to be a lot harder than he intended to find Luna, but he figures that he has to try. In a moment of panic, he squeezes the communication device embedded in his wrist, which is luckily still there for the time being, until it is expelled from his body. He whispers into it.

"Locate Luna."

But then he remembers that hers was expelled days ago, and the chances of it still working were slim to none. Despite what he knows to be true, he tries to locate her with his embedded device anyway.

LUNA LOCATED APPROXIMATELY 500 YARDS FROM CURRENT LOCATION.

By some miracle, it appears that though expelled, her tracker is still working, and might be near her. It is a long shot but Onyx follows the tiny, barely visible map that appears on his own inner wrist, leading him to her. Of course, he has to keep this advanced technology away from the wandering eyes of humans, as arousing suspicion is the last thing he needs if he ever hopes to assimilate into society.

Within a few moments, the map on his wrist leads him into what he remembers learning was the emergency room, with many people rushing around tending to various medical problems. There are many curtained-off areas housing various patients, and he knows he is getting close. And then, just about ten feet away, he sees her, sleeping, but alive. And there is a faint, blurry blue light emanating from a plastic bag on a bedside table next to where she lay.

"Hello? Luna? Luna!"

Onyx rushes over to her side, finally living the reunion that he had craved for so long. Although, in his most desperate dreams to find her again, he never considered the possibility that she would be unconscious, or worse yet, dead.

"Excuse me? Who are you?"

Onyx turns around abruptly to see a human boy standing up from the chair he was sitting in at the foot of Luna's bed, with a small girl cowering behind him. Both had very curly blond hair, and faces filled with nothing but fear and confusion.

"Anthony, who is this guy?" The boy draws the small girl closer to himself, protecting her from this potential safety breach.

"I don't know, Felicia. Yet." He wastes no more time and locks eyes with Onyx.

"Who... who are you? And what are you doing here?"

Onyx shifts his glance from Luna, the girl he's been thinking about nonstop since the moment her molecules were scrambled in the transport room, to the mysterious human who is staring him down.

"My name is Onyx. I'm here to see Luna. I'm... responsible for her, so to speak."

Anthony's cheeks begin to turn a rosy red, but not because he is embarrassed. Rather, he is *jealous*.

"What do you mean, you're *responsible* for her? I've taken her into my home, and helped her, even when she was… expecting an unwanted child. I already take care of my little sister alone, but Luna was someone who needed help and a place to stay, so I gave it to her, simple as that. Where have *you* been?" His words seethed behind his clenched teeth, his hand balled into a fist at his side.

"I've been…" Onyx searches for the right explanation, but finds none to explain his absence, besides being in the Upperworld. That detail must not be revealed to a human, it's too far beyond their limits of consciousness.

"That's what I thought. You still need to tell me who you are though." Anthony begins to settle down, but crosses his arms as if to punctuate his point.

"Well, if you must know, I am her intended life partner."

Anthony raises his eyebrows. "Oh really? Interesting. Now tell me, *Onyx*, does she really know you? Or are you just some sicko looking to get some action from a sick girl in a hospital?"

"What? I don't know what you mean…"

"But you still haven't told me how you know her or why you're really here."

"I'll show you…"

Anthony opens his mouth to speak, but closes it as Felicia quietly pulls at his sleeve to get his attention, and then wraps her arms around his waist. He takes her silent cue to sit down, and places her gently on his lap.

Onyx moves slowly toward the bed where Luna is.

"She's only sleeping, correct?"

Anthony nods.

Onyx carefully strokes her pale forehead, gently brushing away the dark tendrils of her unbrushed-hair.

"Luna, I've missed you *so* much…"

He gently taps her on the shoulder, but she is in a deep sleep and does not awaken at even his gentle touch. And then he remembers, the last thing he did before her body disappeared in the transport room - it might be just the thing to wake her up. It was something he had studied decades ago during his training to be a Primary Guide, some typical social commonality that humanoids would participate in, likely in response to elevated hormones and emotional desire.

The thoughts of all the scientific logistics flood his head, but they dissipate the moment his lips touch hers in a passionate embrace. He only meant to quickly jolt her awake, but she fills him with the warmest, internal feeling of consummate satisfaction he'd ever known in his over four hundred years of existence, and he couldn't stop, until her brilliant violet eyes open for him once again.

"Onyx?" She breathes softly, her petite chest rising and falling in the wake of both medical trauma and romantic excitement.

"I'm here now, Luna."

Her pale, frail hand reaches up to touch the smoothest skin on his cheek, his bright blue eyes locked with hers. And then Luna slowly sits up on the hospital bed, ignoring the pain from her aching bruises and breaks, and pulls Onyx's face to her own. She isn't usually one to be this aggressively forward, but Onyx is her one and only. And he accepts her advances wholeheartedly.

"Okay, *clearly* you two know each other, I stand corrected", Anthony rolls his eyes and stares out into the bustling emergency room.

"Anthony, what are they doing?"

"I'll tell you when you're older, Fel." He shields her eyes gingerly with the palm of his hand even though she pushes it away with her own small, but deliberate, fingers.

A few minutes pass, but to Luna, they're a small eternity until she breaks their powerful kiss for some air.

"Onyx, I needed you…"

"I know, I'm here now."

"Don't let me go alone… I'm scared."

"I know, I saw everything…"

"It was terrible…"

Short sentences like this fly between the two reunited souls after their long time apart. Throughout their conversation, Onyx eases himself onto Luna's small hospital bed, carefully avoiding various wires and her intravenous tube. He reaches behind her heaving back, and pulls her close so that his stronger, brave embrace comforts her small, timid body.

"Well, I'm just going to take Felicia to find some food, she hasn't eaten since dinner last night. We'll be back, Luna." But Luna fails to see the wistful look in Anthony's eyes as he looks back at her while leading Felicia out into the hallway - Luna is far too lost in thought and perfect rapture in Onyx's arms.

CHAPTER 8

Miranda exits the bus and makes her way through the parking lot and into the main entrance of the hospital. She isn't feeling too well herself - a nasty break-up and a steady diet of nothing but frosting and cookie dough could do that to a girl. But for some unknown reason, even to herself, she is determined to make sure Anthony is okay. That is, she is assuming that he is the one *in* the hospital, injured. He must have called in to get off work - or worse yet, maybe someone had to on his behalf. Although she doesn't know him all that well, Miranda has nothing better to do and feels a rather strange inclination to check on him. With all these thoughts swirling through her head, she gets to the reception desk and asks for her acquaintance-friend.

"Excuse me, could you tell me where I can find Anthony Stevens? I was notified by his boss that he had been here."

The receptionist adjusts her garish, black-rimmed glasses and then rapidly types on her concealed keyboard.

"I don't have a patient under that name, do you think you are mistaken, Miss?"

"No, I think I would know who I came to see."

"Well, he isn't a patient here. If he was, his name would be in the database. Sorry." And that is the extent of her apology - she quickly reverts back to reading the latest issue of some gaudy fashion magazine.

"Well thanks for nothing", Miranda mumbles under her breath. She walks away from the main desk, but refuses to give up and go home just yet. Until she figures out how to find Anthony, the rumbling in her stomach prompts her to embark on a search for some new junk food in the cafeteria to numb the pain from her heartache.

She matches the rhythm of her steps to her heartbeat and breathes deeply, trying to steady her nerves to avoid a panic attack in the middle of the hospital (even if that might be the ideal spot for a panic attack, it was still extremely unpleasant and embarrassing).

Miranda is about five steps away from the churro kiosk when she runs into someone.

"Hey - watch where you're going, jerk!"

"Oh, I'm sorry…"

She recognizes that voice immediately, especially in the context of buying junk food.

"Anthony? What are you doing out of your room? How are you feeling?"

"What? My room? I'm fine, I don't have a room because I don't need one… what are you talking about?"

Miranda exhales deeply.

"Oh, I could've sworn your boss said you were in the hospital? I was out of frosting, so I went to the mini-mart and you weren't there…"

Anthony sighs. "Yeah, I'm here because the girl I took in, who needed a place to stay, was randomly hit by a truck in the middle of the night, and she sustained some broken bones and bruising. She's going to be fine, but needs to mend a bit first."

Miranda nods. "Oh, right, Luna, is it? She's a very sweet girl, I was horrified at what she told me about... Garth. Completely shocked. I've since dumped his sorry ass and threatened to personally castrate him myself if he ever tries to violate someone like that ever again. He's the scum of Earth and I'm just ashamed I ever gave him the time of day..."

Anthony politely nods through her post-breakup tirade, but his heart aches from the realization that his feelings for Luna definitely did not seem mutual. It was selfish, and crazy to get so attached to a girl he barely knew, but he did, and now he's paying the price.

"... So now I've just been sitting at home, counting dust bunnies. And there sure are a lot of them, especially now."

"Well, I'm sorry to hear you've been having a hard time, but I really should get Felicia some lunch, so..."

Miranda grabs his hand. "But I've been *so lonely*. I'm glad that you're okay... maybe I can have lunch with you guys?"

Anthony looks down at his little sister. "You know, I think the two of us have just been through a lot recently, and just need a little time -"

"Anthony, it's okay. She can eat with us. You told me to always include anyone who wants to be a friend..." He smiles at his sister's ingenuity and unflappable spirit.

"If you're sure, Fel."

She nods.

"Well, apparently, my sister is feeling more hospitable than I am today. But regardless, sure, we can get lunch together."

Miranda stopped fighting the smile threatening to turn up the corners of her mouth, and allowed herself to radiate the nearly heavenly warmth that instantly filled her body. Anthony suddenly begins to smile too.

The two of them make their way over to a sandwich kiosk, with Felicia tagging along next to them both. An onlooker might view them as a couple with a young child, had they not heard either of their stories.

And at that moment, the lives torn apart by a terrible blunder come back together. It was merely lunch, but in this case it was the beginning of the erasure of a mistake. Two lives broken are whole once again, and Luna would have been able to return to the Sorting Room at this point, if it wasn't for the revolution threatening to break out at any moment.

CHAPTER 9

"Delphine, honey? You've been in front of that TV all day... how about a nice walk outside?"

Delphine peels her eyes away from the brightly-lit screen, and tries her best to give her caretaker the attention that she knows she rightfully deserves.

"Oh, um, okay..."

"There's a handy little convenience store right down the street, why don't you get yourself a soda or a treat? Here's some cash."

Delphine nods graciously, but suddenly gets a bad feeling in the pit of her stomach at the prospect of going outside. She decides to ignore it, and walks outside anyway. But she quickly realizes that was a mistake.

The bright sun in the perfect cerulean sky beats down on her pale shoulders, and her black tank top seems to instantly radiate the heat. Her skin reacts immediately, and a slight rash begins to appear, and with it, burning, searing pain. She drops to her knees, but feeling weakened, crawls back inside the house as quickly as she can.

"Delphine, are you okay? Why are you crawling?"

"The... sunlight hurts me. Look." Delphine holds out her arm to show Elizabeth the irritated flesh. "I'm not sure why it did that but it hurts."

"That is so strange... that's never happened to me. Maybe I should take you to a doctor?"

"No!"

Elizabeth frowns slightly but nods.

"Maybe not for this. Doctors here don't know how to treat beings from another realm. Although I've never seen anything like it, it's probably not impossible. Perhaps it's just you adapting to the stress and the different climate."

"So I'm okay?"

"I think so. We'll just have to keep an eye on it. There's no telling what could happen, if it keeps showing up and we don't do anything about it."

"And can I go back to watching TV?" Elizabeth sighs.

"At the moment, there's nothing else I would suggest to you. Alright."

Delphine smiles sheepishly and walks calmly toward the living room.

"But I'm going to put some ointment on that burn, just in case."

"Some what?"

"Just a soothing balm to make it feel better."

Elizabeth spreads the thick, white gel over Delphine's arms and shoulders, and then retreats back to her home office to continue working. But the thought that occurred to her wouldn't quit.

I doubt she could have really been a sorter with that strange reaction... I don't want to scare her but I believe that she has been lied to. Perhaps I should contact Evander...

After checking to make sure that the blinds are closed, and that her laptop camera is obscured, she taps the communication device that she had permanently reinstalled under her skin upon taking on the responsibility for Delphine. It makes communication with the Upperworld quick and easy, and the fact that it cannot be traced like Earthly phones is critical to her cause. Of course, it wasn't easy finding a surgeon that knew of such a device, much less that would be willing implant one, but Evander was kind enough to direct her to a friend of his that worked in the Galapagos Islands, who runs an underground medical practice for high-tech body modifications. This device is linked directly to her circulatory system, so it cannot be expelled by her body.

After a few moments, Elizabeth hears Evander answer her call.

"Hi, Evander... Yes, she is doing fine. I just noticed something quite strange... you see, I sent her outside for some fresh air and a short walk to the convenience store, but she complained that the sun burned her... No, not like a sunburn. Like an immediate burning. She was out there for maybe thirty seconds before she came back in here with a nasty rash on her arms and shoulders... WHAT? You don't say... does anyone else know about this? Okay, okay. Does she know? Yeah I think I'd rather not tell her. I'm perfectly happy to take care of her myself for as long as she needs... I never could have kids on my own so I'd rather like that, actually. I just wish I knew about this sooner... How did this happen? Wow. Okay. Thank you, Evander."

She pinches her own wrist gently to end the call, and then sits back in her office chair, taking a few cleansing breaths.

A demon? How could this happen?

EPILOGUE

"Onyx... you won't ever leave me again, right?"

Onyx shakes his head, while gently caressing the side of Luna's face.

"Never again. I can't imagine... what you've been through. I'm glad you're... alive."

He leans over her and kisses her again, but this time, just for a moment, as he can sense that the onslaught of emotions rushing through her brain is quickly tiring her out.

"Can... can... we go home now?"

Onyx looks in the direction of Luna's pointed finger, where Anthony and Miranda walk down the hall together, with Felicia in tow.

"They're finally together now..."

Onyx smiles slightly, but has trouble searching for the right words to explain to her what was happening.

"They are, and that is fantastic news. But... there's something else you should know..."

Luna's large, violet eyes stare back into his with anticipation.

"What?"

Onyx breathes deeply before continuing his explanation. He knows the next words out of his mouth are going to scare her, likely even more than her terrifying experiences on Earth.

"The system is breaking apart... and you're being chased."

"By who? Is someone following me?" She immediately sits up straighter, gritting her teeth against the pain in her rib cage from her accident.

"No, don't get up. I need you to stay calm. No one is after you… yet. But he's coming, and I bet it's only a matter of time before he finds you."

"What? Who?"

Onyx gently places his strong hand over Luna's still slightly swollen abdomen. To the untrained eye, her pregnancy wasn't obvious. And it ended nearly as quickly as it began. But her body still held the signs of her attack, and the attacker's fingerprints left scars on her consciousness that would remain as long as she lives.

"The baby… isn't gone."

"But the nurse told me it was."

"Well, okay, in this realm, it is gone. But it ended up in the Upperworld. I *saw him* myself." And Zephyr's using him to… destroy you." Onyx chokes on the words, willing everything in his power to make the reality of it untrue. But he knows that is impossible, because like it or not, Luna is in deep trouble for trying to return to the Upperworld and allowing Delphine to take her place on Earth. At least, that is how Zephyr viewed the situation. In reality, it was Onyx's plotting to get her home that likely caused suspicion, especially when Jade meant well, but ended up blurting out everything to the Most High Being of the Upperworld, who would waste no time in exacting his revenge.

236

Luna barely responds. She just buries her face in Onyx's shoulder, and cries. She cries for fear of being caught. She cries because she's tired of running.

"When... and where... will I go?"

Onyx pulls her closer, wrapping his arm around her trembling shoulders. They both stare at the sunlight pouring through the windows, a completely ironic display of joy in the path of utter destruction.

"Well, I'm not going anywhere, so you can stay with me. And I, myself, will protect you."

"But how? I don't know anything about this place, and I've been here, for a little while. You can help me?"

Onyx brushes some hair out of her face soothingly, and then lowers his own voice down to a whisper in order to keep their abnormal reality a secret from the unwitting ears of the other patients and caretakers in the hospital.

"You may have forgotten, but I've studied Earth life extensively for my guide position. I know this stuff. Of course, I don't have experience living on Earth, but I know enough about it to figure it out as I go. I'll protect you, Luna. I will make it my mission to protect you as long as I live."

"But... what if *he* finds me?"

"Well, I think he should be more afraid of us finding *him*. Because I will defend you at all costs, and it won't end well for him. Now get some sleep - I know it's scary, but I'll be right here. You have to heal. Then I'll make arrangements for us."

Onyx leaves one chaste kiss on her forehead, and then gets up off of the hospital bed and situates himself in the nearby chair.

Anthony and Miranda re-enter the curtained-off area where Luna was sleeping, with Felicia in tow, nibbling on a giant chocolate chip cookie.

"So yeah, I mean, we should... do this again sometime." Anthony raises an eyebrow at Miranda's suggestion.

"You mean, accidentally meet up in a hospital after someone I know gets in an accident?" She giggles like a schoolgirl in response.

"No, silly. I meant we should... hang out more. I have like, no life since I broke up with that asshat. I'm actually ashamed how much I let him get into my life. Without him, without the band, I've got nothing."

Anthony slowly nods, and then looks over at Onyx, who sits calmly on a hospital chair next to Luna's bed.

"I'm sorry, I don't believe you ever told me who you are?"

"I am Onyx."

"And why are you here, again?"

"I am here for Luna."

"And why is that?"

"Because I will be taking care of her from now on."

Anthony smirks. "Yeah I certainly saw you 'taking care' of her earlier. So, what are you, her boyfriend? Husband? Lover?"

Onyx pauses for a moment to register what those terms mean in the context of human colloquialism.

"Something like that, yes."

"And you expect me to just let you take her away? I don't know you, what if you hurt her like she's been hurt before?"

Onyx winces at the thought of Luna being attacked days ago, as he had the unfortunate opportunity to witness it in real time from the Sorting Room monitor.

"I would *never* do that to her."

"Is that so?"

Miranda taps Anthony on the shoulder.

"Anthony, if he seems to be someone she knows, then that sounds fine. You've done all you can for her. It's probably for the best that she lives with him now." Anthony hesitates, but then nods slowly, understanding filling his face.

Felicia tugs on his sleeve the way she always does when she wants his attention.

"Anthony, what's happening now?" He crouches down to her level.

"Well, it seems that Luna is going to live with her friend... uh, Onyx."

"Why?"

"Because he loves her."

"And you don't?"

Anthony smiles awkwardly at Miranda, and then shakes off the discomfort and puts on a brave face the way any big brother should, even when pinpointed with his most recent source of insecurity.

"I care about Luna's well-being, if that's what you mean. And I think this is best for her. That's love, Felicia." She nods contentedly, but looks over her shoulder at Onyx sitting on the chair reading a magazine.

"The way you just said that to her, was so sweet." Miranda links her arm up with Anthony's, a subtle nod to a possible relationship. He doesn't realize it yet, but Miranda is his *one and only*, just the way Luna is Onyx's.

JOURNEY BACK TO
THE UPPERWORLD
BEFORE IT IS
DESTROYED
FOREVER...

THE FALL OF
ZEPHYR

THE SEQUEL TO
THE SORTING ROOM
COMING SOON IN 2018

Exclusive Sneak Peak:

The lavender-tinted atmosphere of the Upperworld parts as two beings march through the fog in a desperate haste. Their footfalls hit the ground and cascade over their surroundings, which is surprisingly disruptive in the already bustling walkway. Evander and Jade enter a habitation pod and begin to discuss their latest source of sheer terror – directly related to the only life they've ever known.

Since the drastic confusion involving Delphine, a young sorter who placed an orb into the wrong receptacle, and the involvement of Luna covering for her blunder, there have been concerns that the very mechanisms involving the operations of the Sorting Room are falling apart.

Luna's story, is a complicated one, as she and her intended partner, Onyx, were both meant to live human lives on Earth, but due to circumstances beyond even the Sorting Room's control, their souls were retracted back into the larger sorting system, and given the opportunity to work as immortal beings. The only problem, is that their very human attributes took over, and they still loved each other, even after their minds were wiped. Luna tried to fix Delphine's horrible mistake on Earth, but ended up with a scorned child of her own… and now that very child was chasing her, ensuring her demise at the request of Zephyr, the Most High Being of the Upperworld.

"We need a new leader, Evander. We've got to appoint someone. And soon. The future of humanity depends on it."

"What are you talking about? How? But Zephyr…"

"Is dying. His ability to map out life schemes and generate orbs are becoming less and less accurate. It's a miracle that there haven't been any more mix-ups, besides the one with Luna covering for Delphine."

Evander holds his face in his hands. "I know, but this is… crazy. There's nothing we can do. We need… a fail-safe, or something we can get to just to keep fear at a minimum."

Jade nods. "That is very true. We also need a way to explain Onyx's absence in the meantime…"

"Do you think you'll be able to cover for him? If anyone asks, maybe say that he…"

"Has a mission on Earth - yes, that could work."

"But what if Zephyr asks you? He's going to find out eventually - Onyx is a Head Guide."

Jade nods her head. "It's true, I think there's just a lot we have to account for. I also worry that these walls have ears."

Evander shakes his head. "Nope, not anymore. I neutralized my habitation pod to be a dead zone. There are no cameras or sound recordings being transmitted beyond these walls. We can use this as a safe place to talk… and to plan."

"We're going to need to rally sorters for the cause."

"And the cause being?"

"Two things: to take down Zephyr, and to elect a new leader. I have no idea who that could be, or how we'll figure it out…"

Evander looks at Jade with horror and dread in his eyes. "But… will the new leader be able to lead? Will they have the ability to generate orbs? If they don't, the human race…"

"Will go extinct."

ANGELINA SINGER is a college student studying English, Music, and of course, Creative Writing. In her spare time she enjoys crocheting, and mentoring younger music students at a local music store where she has been studying guitar for nearly a decade. She views her writing as a way to simultaneously escape from and embrace reality, especially through the twisted labyrinth of a dystopian setting as seen in *The Sorting Room*.

Follow her on Faceobok @AngelinaSingerAuthor

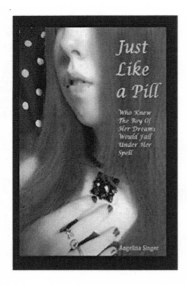

Made in the USA
Middletown, DE
30 September 2021